D0407479

DESTINY ARRIVES

WRITTEN BY LIZA PALMER

Los Angeles • New York

© 2019 MARVEL

First Edition, April 2019
10 9 8 7 6 5 4 3 2 1
FAC-020093-19046
Printed in the United States of America
This book is set in Agmena Pro

Designed by Catalina Castro
Cover illustration by Lente Scura
Illustrations by Steve Kurth

Library of Congress Control Number: 2018962993
ISBN 978-1-368-05022-7

Visit www.DisneyBooks.com
and www.Marvel.com

SUSTAINABLE FORESTRY INITIATIVE

Certified Sourcing
www.sfiprogram.org
SFI-00993

THIS LABEL APPLIES TO TEXT STOCK

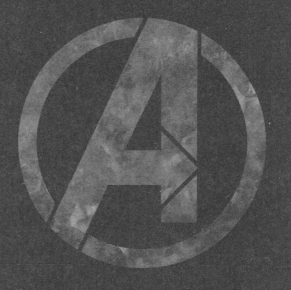

144

PART ONE

CHAPTER 1

Hovering dead in space, the ship was ablaze. Lights were blinking on and off as its power systems began to fail. A voice called out to anyone who could hear them, pleading for help. Begging for mercy.

"This is the Asgardian refugee vessel *Statesman*. We are under assault. I repeat, we are under assault! The engines are dead, life support is failing. Requesting aid from any vessel within range. We are twenty-two jump points out of Asgard."

The ship responsible for the destruction of the *Statesman* dwarfed the vessel, menacing as it hung, its curved wings enveloping them. The colossal ship was the *Sanctuary II*— the base of the galactic "Mad Titan," Thanos.

"Our crew is made up of Asgardian families. We have very few soldiers here. This is not a war craft. I repeat, this is *not* a war craft."

Aboard the *Statesman*, a figure emerged from the destruction.

"Hear me, and rejoice."

Ebony Maw strolled through the wreckage. His flat, elongated face had sunken eyes and wide lips that stretched across a mouth that rarely smiled. Tufts of white hair swept down the back of his head. His tight black robes were trimmed in gold, and these, along with his dark pants and heavy boots, left only his face and hands visible. He pressed his hands together, his long fingertips touching gently, as pale and wrinkled as his face. His voice was unnervingly soothing given the chaos that surrounded him.

"You have had the privilege of being saved by the Great Titan."

He stepped over several bodies, all badly wounded. "You may think this is suffering."

Heimdall, former keeper of the Bifrost, grunted, bloodied and bruised as he tried to lift himself. Blood ran in his eye as he collapsed back down, mentally praying to Odin and the All-Fathers of old.

"No." Ebony Maw looked to the heavens, his voice raised. "It is *salvation*."

As Ebony Maw ambled among the dead and dying, the remainder of the Black Guard followed behind, putting those clinging to life out of their misery once and for all. Considered his "siblings," they were all found and raised by Thanos, taken from their home worlds as the Titan continued his march across the galaxy on a mission. A mission that only he and his disciples could fathom as just and noble. There was Proxima Midnight, her horned head and deep-set eyes glowering as she held her electric staff, charged and crackling. The lithe Corvus Glaive, looking like a dark hooded elf, held his double-ended spear by his side, ready for a fight. Cull Obsidian's huge frame dominated above them all, deadly techno-hammer gripped in his hands as he snarled, his scaly skin and bone-ridged head striking fear into the survivors who dared look upon him.

"Universal scales tip toward balance because of your sacrifice." Ebony Maw looked into the eyes of a gravely wounded Asgardian, his face softening. "Smile," he said, as the dying woman heaved her last breath. "For even in death, you have become Children of Thanos."

Ebony Maw joined the Black Guard as they surrounded their prisoner—Loki, the God of Mischief himself.

Loki gave Ebony Maw a withering stare when Maw was finally done pontificating, but then slid his gaze to the figure that loomed above all else. The figure that these enemies called "Father": Thanos. His purple hide-like skin was covered in battle armor, his helmed head revealing cold, dispassionate eyes. And for the first time in his life, Loki decided to remain silent.

"I know what it's like to lose," came Thanos's measured, gravelly voice as he looked down at the wary, yet still defiant Loki. "To feel so desperately that you're right, yet to fail nonetheless."

Thanos looked down at the broken and battered figure at his feet and lifted Thor from the ground as if he were a rag doll. Then, Thanos effortlessly closed the space between him and Loki, while holding a squirming Thor closer to his adoptive brother.

"It's frightening. Turns the legs to jelly. But, I ask you,

to what end? Dread it. Run from it. Destiny arrives all the same. And now it's here. Or should I say, I am."

Thanos dramatically lifted his hand to reveal that it was gloved in gleaming gold: the Infinity Gauntlet. Forged with six settings, one on each knuckle and a larger one on the back of the hand. Each setting was designed to hold an Infinity Stone, one of which he already possessed. The violet glow of the Power Stone pulsed as he flexed his fist and curled his fingers.

"You talk too much," Thor spat, blood dripping from his mouth. Loki's eyes flicked from Thanos to Thor, his mind reeling with clever misdirects, resourceful trickery, and possible escape routes.

"The Tesseract." Thanos's voice was matter-of-fact. "Or your brother's head. I assume you have a preference." Loki's face remained strategically expressionless as he appeared to weigh Thanos's proposition.

"Oh, I do," said the God of Mischief, his voice daring. "Kill away."

Thanos bit back his surprise at Loki's apparent indifference to his adoptive brother, and without breaking eye contact, he tightened his hand into a fist, and placed the Infinity Gauntlet on the side of Thor's face. The Power Stone lit up upon contact, and smoke instantly began to rise off Thor's searing flesh.

As Thor's cries echoed through the broken craft, Loki's false bravado faltered. He shook and battled to stay in control of his emotions, positive Thor could withstand any punishment, as he'd done so many times before. But Thor's heightening screams quickly became unbearable, and Loki came to realize how wrong he'd been. As Thanos looked on, Loki's red-rimmed eyes flashed in fear. This was not like those other times. He could endure this no longer.

"All right, stop!" Loki yelled, his voice a frustrated roar.

Thanos removed his hand, and the Stone dulled. Loki closed his eyes and breathed a sigh of relief at Thor's now quieted screams. His head still gripped in the Titan's vise-like hand, Thor coughed an explanation at Thanos. "We don't have the Tesseract. It was destroyed on Asgard."

Loki looked up with an expression Thor knew all too well. Thor looked in horror as his half-brother lifted his hand and the gleaming blue cube that was the Tesseract appeared from thin air. Thanos smiled as Thor flared with his one good eye. "You really are the worst brother," Thor sighed.

For his part, however, Loki remained confident, walking to Thanos, Tesseract in hand. His voice was steely and resolved. "I assure you, Brother, the sun will shine on us again."

Loki halted, steps away from delivering the Tesseract

to Thanos, his face resolute. Thanos gave him a cold stare and laughed.

"Your optimism is misplaced, Asgardian."

Loki lifted his chin stubbornly. His mouth curled into that know-it-all grin. "Well, for one thing, I'm not Asgardian. And for another . . ." His eyes lit up as the trickster god revealed the ace up his sleeve.

"We have a Hulk."

At that, Loki dropped the Tesseract and dove toward Thor, pulling him to safety. With three loud *THUD*s, the Hulk charged from the side of the ship, leaped, and slammed into Thanos, knocking the giant figure against the wall. The crumbling ship shook as the two collided. Thanos hit the floor with an audible grunt. Hulk faced Thanos and let out a battle cry.

Hulk bounded toward the stunned Thanos and waylaid him with a series of powerful blows. Then he wrapped his hands around Thanos's neck and drove him deep into the *Statesman*'s charred and crumbling walls. Cull Obsidian, seeing his "father" in distress, moved to intercept the Hulk, wanting to test his own massive strength against the green goliath, but Ebony Maw stopped the brute with a simple hand gesture.

"Let him have his fun," said Maw knowingly.

Thanos grabbed Hulk's wrists, peeled his hands away from his neck, and landed a mighty punch to Hulk's own

neck. Stunned by Thanos's incomparable strength, the Avenger howled in pain and frustration; the tide turned with every blow Thanos threw.

Thanos, having dazed the Hulk, grabbed him and hoisted him above his head in a single swift motion. With a wicked grin, Thanos slammed the stupefied hero to the floor. Seeing his friend in trouble, Thor painfully rose to his feet, grabbing a pipe. Just as Thanos was about to land a destructive blow, Thor swung the pipe, hitting the Titan across the back with a weak and embarrassing *THWOOP*.

Retaliating, Thanos moved faster than Thor believed possible, pivoting on one foot and kicking the Thunder God squarely in the chest, sending him flying. Thor landed in the middle of twisted metal, wreckage from the limping ship. With a fluid gesture, Ebony Maw used his telekinesis to bend the metal around the Asgardian, binding him in place.

Heimdall scanned the carnage grimly from where he lay splayed out across the deck, mortally wounded but still alive, though luckily none of the Children of Thanos had seemed to notice as of yet. Thanos was unlike any enemy they'd battled, and he knew he must do something before it was too late. Bravely summoning his last ounce of strength, Heimdall reached for his beloved sword, Hofund, one last time. As he clung to the last threads of life, his voice choked and stuttered. Riddled with pain, he closed his all-seeing eyes in prayer and spoke, "All-Fathers, let the dark magic flow through me one last time."

Hand on hilt, his palm began to glow. Before Thanos or the Children of Thanos could react, the rainbow energy of the Bifrost filled the ship and formed into a tunnel that enveloped the battered Hulk. In a bright blaze, the jade behemoth vanished, carried through the failing *Statesman* out into deep space, where the Bifrost arced and traveled at faster-than-light speeds through the galaxy. Heimdall's body fell, drained and relieved. The Hulk was saved.

Thanos turned to Heimdall, the Asgardian fully aware that he would not find the same salvation. He glared at Thanos, judging the villain as he approached the fallen Keeper of the Bifrost.

"That was a mistake," Thanos said, gripping Corvus Glaive's cruel-looking double-ended spear. Heimdall met Thor's eyes one last time, knowing his fate was sealed. Thor could only look on in helpless horror as Heimdall turned his gaze back to Thanos, who had lifted the spear high above his friend's weak and unprotected body. But Heimdall's eyes were bold and unwavering as Thanos plunged the spear into the Asgardian's chest.

"No!" Thor struggled against his metallic restraints, furious. His voice rattled in rage as Thanos twisted the spear deeper into Heimdall's now lifeless body. "You're . . . going to . . . *die* for that," Thor sputtered. But even with flexing his mighty muscles, Thor still couldn't get free of his bonds. He saw Ebony Maw flick his wrist once more, and a piece of salvage slammed against Thor's mouth, muffling his words to agonized grunts.

"Shh," Maw instructed calmly with a snide look.

Ebony Maw strode to the fallen Tesseract. Awestruck, he held it in his hands, the very cube that had driven people mad by the mere whispers of power it seemed to usher, filling the heads of less-willful beings. But Maw had long ago submitted to the fact that there was only one true power in the Universe: his master and adoptive father, to whom he now presented the Tesseract.

"My humble personage bows before your grandeur." Ebony Maw knelt before Thanos, lowering his head in reverence. In preparation to finally be in possession of the Tesseract, Thanos took off his helmet and armored breastplate. Maw lifted the cube with his spindly arms as Thanos loomed over him. "No other being has ever had the might, nay, the *nobility* to wield not one, but two Infinity Stones."

One step closer to completing his mission, Thanos took the Tesseract rapturously from his humble servant's hands. He held it in his palm, awed and quieted by its power.

"The universe lies within your grasp," Maw's voice praised.

Suddenly, Thanos's massive hand closed around the cube and shattered it in a brilliant blaze. Opening his hand, he blew away the shards to reveal a gleaming oval Stone, the purest blue ever seen since the dawn of time itself.

The Space Stone pulsed radiant energy in its new master's hand.

Thanos deftly danced the Stone in his hands before gently holding it with his thumb and index finger. He raised his right hand, the gleaming Infinity Gauntlet shining. The Space Stone's "sibling," the Power Stone, began to vibrate in its place on the index knuckle. Thanos gently dropped the Space Stone into the slot on his middle knuckle and was immediately awash in luminous blue energy.

With two Infinity Stones in his possession, Thanos seemed to stand even more formidably than he had a moment ago, if that was possible. He flexed the Gauntlet and smiled in satisfaction. He turned to face the Children of Thanos.

"There are two more Stones on Earth." His baritone voice reverberated across the ship. "Find them, my children, and bring them to me on Titan."

Proxima Midnight dipped her horned head. "Father, we will not fail you," she vowed. Corvus Glaive and Cull Obsidian mirrored their sister's bow of acknowledgment.

Before they could leave, a tentative voice interrupted. "If I might interject," said Loki in a smooth and deceptively playful tone, "if you're going to Earth, you might want a guide." He smiled. "I do have a bit of experience in that arena."

"If you consider failure experience," Thanos taunted. He hadn't forgotten Loki's foiled attempt to take over New York with the aid of Thanos's Chitauri warriors six years earlier.

Loki squared off with Thanos and spoke emphatically. "I consider experience experience."

Corvus Glaive moved his lithe body to intercept, but Thanos waved him off. Loki continued. "Almighty Thanos," he said, voice filling with confidence, "I, Loki, prince of Asgard . . ." Loki trailed off. His bravado stripped away momentarily as his body softened. His next words were intimate and unguarded. "Odinson." Loki looked to Thor, trapped and muted, who could only watch in horror as Loki spun what was surely an elaborate and tangled web of trickery and swagger.

Loki continued walking toward the Titan. "The rightful king of Jotunheim, God of Mischief." Thanos missed the glint of a knife hidden in Loki's hand. But Thor saw it. His eyes flared with warning and worry and rage at his adoptive brother's flagrant stupidity and his inability to read this enemy as something worthy of more than Loki's usual parlor tricks. And perhaps a touch of admiration at his brother's bravery, no matter how naïve. "Do hereby pledge to you my undying fidelity." Loki took a deep, steadying breath and then, with blinding speed, he lunged at Thanos, knife held high . . . only to be stopped in midair, frozen in place by the Power Stone.

Thanos's eyes narrowed. "Undying?" The Titan mused as he gripped Loki's wrist. Twisting it, the knife fell from the would-be assassin's grip as bones cracked.

"You should choose your words more carefully," Thanos chuckled. In an instant, the gauntleted hand was around Loki's neck, squeezing the life from him. Thanos's calculating, icy eyes watched as Loki twisted in agony, face turning blue.

Loki's miscalculation had another heartbroken witness. Disbelieving and utterly unable to help, Thor's entire being cracked from within as all he could do was watch, powerless to step in and save his younger brother one last time. Loki croaked out his final words: "You will never be . . . a god." Whether it was a threat or a premonition, Thanos would never know. Nor, it seemed, did he care to find out, as he continued to tighten his grip.

Thor's muffled screams rose above his half-brother's dying gasps. As Loki's body went limp, Thanos walked Loki's now lifeless corpse closer to Thor, callously holding his now-dead adoptive brother up for closer inspection. Thor struggled to come to terms with whether this was real. Loki had "died" several times before, Thor reasoned, starting to panic. This time would be like all the rest. Loki was just playing his games. He would come back. Thor desperately studied his brother's body, looking for any signs of life, any imperceptible wink or smirk. But there was nothing.

Nothing.

No . . . this . . . this couldn't be happening. Sheer terror shot through Thor's body as Thanos casually tossed Loki's body to the ground. He landed near Thor, who choked out a heart-wrenching "NO!"

"No resurrections this time," Thanos stated plainly to Thor. Loki's broken, motionless body echoed that claim.

Thanos raised his hand and the Stones in the Infinity Gauntlet glowed as he made a fist. A black vortex formed behind the Children of Thanos. They stepped through it, disappearing. As soon as Ebony Maw had vanished, the metal shackling Thor clattered to the ground, as did the Asgardian himself.

Thanos gave him one last look, and Thor met his gaze, murder in his eyes. But before Thor could muster the strength to rise, Thanos was gone, the teleportation energy vanishing with him.

Thor crawled to his brother, pulling Loki's lifeless body closer to him. "No, Loki," he cried, softly. "No." Thor let his head fall onto Loki's chest and sobbed, finally coming to terms with the fact that this time, there were no games, no second or third or fourth chances.

Loki was dead. And there was nothing Thor could have done to stop it.

As Thor mourned his brother, the *Sanctuary II* opened fire on the remains of the *Statesman* from the inky darkness beyond. Fires flared as the missiles impacted the ship, ripping it apart. A silent explosion tore the remains of the once-great ship apart, scattering debris and fallen Asgardians across empty space.

Its job finished, the *Sanctuary II* vanished.

Many light-years away, the Bifrost sped past a glowing star as it carried the Hulk along its intergalactic track. Impossibly fast, it turned past a familiar-looking orbital moon and aimed itself at the blue-and-green planet below.

Earth.

A stately manor graced Bleecker Street in New York City's Greenwich Village. To the unsuspecting passersby, it was an old Victorian building. But to a precious few, it was known by its actual name: the Sanctum Sanctorum, home to the Master of the Mystic Arts: Doctor Stephen Strange.

"Seriously? You don't have any money?" Strange asked his fellow Master of the Mystic Arts, Wong. Both Wong and Strange were tasked with acting as guardians to the New York Sanctum.

"Attachment to the material is detachment from the spiritual," Wong said, trailing after Strange as they descended the sweeping staircase of the Sanctum.

"I'll tell the guys at the deli. Maybe they'll make you a metaphysical ham on rye." Strange trotted down the stairs, dressed in a gray sweatshirt and a loose black coat, hands tucked casually into his jeans pockets.

"Oh. Wait, wait, wait, wait. I think I have two hundred." Wong reached up and scrounged around in the inner lining pocket of his vest. He victoriously pulled out a balled-up scrap of paper money.

"Dollars?" Strange asked, pausing for the slightest moment to entertain what he knew would turn out to be a farce. Wong unfolded the paper money and his whole body deflated.

"Rupees."

"Which amounts to . . . ?" Strange's voice was clipped and annoyed.

"Uh, a buck and a half?" Wong confessed.

Resigned, Strange shook his head and continued down the stairs without looking back, then sighed. "What do you want?" Strange asked, and Wong brightened.

"I wouldn't say no to a tuna melt."

But their metaphysical debate and impending trip

to the corner deli was interrupted as the rainbow of the Bifrost plowed through the massive circular window at the center of the Sanctum. Having reached its final destination, the Bifrost dissolved, leaving behind a massive hole where the central staircase once was, along with its sole passenger.

The Cloak of Levitation had appeared as if from nowhere as Wong and Strange braced themselves against the explosion. Rising from their crouched and protected positions, Wong, Strange, and the Cloak boldly ascended what was left of the stairs. As always, running toward what most people would run from, Wong and Doctor Strange approached the crater and peered in. Shocked, they saw the Hulk, slowly transforming into his human alter ego, Bruce Banner.

Tattered and tousled, Banner had a panicked look in his eye. "Thanos is coming," he proclaimed, terrified. "He's coming!"

Strange and Wong exchanged glances. Turning back to Banner, Doctor Strange asked a question that many before him had asked—and were shaken to their core upon hearing the answer.

"Who?"

CHAPTER 2

"Slow down, slow down. I'll spell it out for you," Tony Stark said, as he tried to catch up with Pepper Potts. The two of them were walking along the trails of Central Park in New York.

"You're totally rambling," Pepper said, rolling her eyes. How many times had she said that to Tony? A hundred times? A thousand? Her mind reeled.

Pepper had known Tony for years . . . loved him for years. This rambling genius who was the only person she could imagine spending the rest of her life with. The realization exhausted her—and then lit up every part of her with absolute, unadulterated joy. He was perfect for her, but sometimes she didn't quite know what that said about her.

She had always been someone who did the right thing, made the safe choice, made sure she lived a very controlled, disciplined life . . . until Tony walked into it. Someone who was her opposite in every possible way. She knew Tony always believed he was doing the right thing. She was also certain he'd never made a safe choice even one time in his life. And, as for Tony Stark living a controlled and disciplined life, nothing could be further from the truth.

Pepper and Tony were different in every way. Except one. They loved each other far beyond where either of their comfort zones were okay. That shared love had always been the real adventure in an already ridiculously dangerous existence.

"No, I'm not," retorted Tony Stark.

"You lost me." Pepper's and Tony's words threaded and intertwined seamlessly together. Their rhythms were so well known to each other that it was hard to tell where one ended and the other began. It was clear that Tony and Pepper loved each other. But it was during times like these that it became even more obvious how much they *liked* each other.

"Look, you know how you're having a dream, and in the dream you gotta pee?" Tony pled his case while wearing an all-black workout outfit, topped with a sweatshirt draped carelessly around his shoulders.

"Yeah," Pepper said. Patient, yet moving things along.

"Okay. And then you're like 'Oh my God! There's no bathrooms. What am I gonna do?'"

"Right."

"'Oh, someone's watching. I'm gonna go in my pants—'"

Pepper cut in before Tony's dream scenario got any more unnecessarily graphic. "And then you wake up and in real life you actually have to pee."

Tony turned and pointed a victorious finger at Pepper, thankful to have someone listening to him who finally spoke Tony Stark. She got him. Why did that surprise him every time?

"Yes!" Tony said, triumphant.

"Yeah . . ."

"Okay." Their words blended and moved over and across each other's as if they were performing some kind of nimble, long-winded symphony being played at double time.

"Everybody has that," Pepper said, laughing.

"Right! That's the point I'm trying to make." Tony came to a stop in front of Pepper. He was breathless, but it wasn't from going a mile a minute—as was his usual way. This breathlessness was brought on by the enormity of the statement that he was about to say out loud for the first time. Out loud to Pepper. The woman he not so secretly couldn't believe he got to have in his life.

He took a breath. "Apropos of that, last night I dreamed . . ." Tony trailed off for the tiniest of seconds. Some things can't be unsaid, and he never thought he'd be this guy, but then he met Pepper. A woman who loved him despite . . . well, him being him. A woman who cared about him long before he declared that he was Iron Man. A woman who had saved him as many times as he had saved the world. There were so many different ways to be a Super Hero to someone.

And now here he was, standing in Central Park blurting out, "We had a kid."

Pepper was quiet. So quiet. Tony pressed on. "It was so real. We named him after your eccentric uncle. What was his name?"

"Right," Pepper said, nodding. Her tone was loving yet skeptical. This was often her tone when talking to Tony.

"Morgan!" Tony couldn't believe he actually remembered. "Morgan."

"So you woke up—"

"Naturally." Tony was never above sliding in a joke even in conversations as serious as this.

"—and thought that we were . . ." Pepper looked up at Tony. Her face open and kind. So gentle.

"Expecting." Just one word. Tony waited. The world stood still.

"Yeah," Pepper said, smiling. Tony's heart soared.

"Yes?" Tony asked.

Pepper shook her head emphatically. "No."

"I had a dream about it. It was so real," Tony argued, as if his dreams were as incontestable as something like fact, not to mention science.

"If you wanted to have a kid—" Pepper turned her attention to the glowing entity on Tony's chest, a miniature ARC reactor firmly planted there. She lovingly untied

125

the sweatshirt from his shoulders, so familiar and comfortable being in his space. "You wouldn't have done that," she said, tapping the RT.

Tony looked down then flashed a sheepish grin, trying to defuse the situation. "I'm glad you brought this up, 'cause it's nothing. It's just a housing unit for nanoparticles," he said, waving his hand dismissively. Pepper shook her head, patiently weathering the same speech Tony always gave when she brought up his reliance on the RT.

"You're not helping your case, okay?" Pepper's voice was playfully sarcastic as she looked up to the heavens and away from the absolutely frustrating man she couldn't help but love—despite the fact that he acted utterly dumbfounded every time she brought up the RT's indelible presence in their lives. For such a genius, Tony Stark could be breathtakingly stupid sometimes.

"No, this is detachable. It's not a—"

"You don't need that." There was the Tony Stark the world knew and then there was the Tony Stark who Pepper knew. The Tony Stark who didn't need the miniature ARC reactor to make him amazing. She wondered why, even with all of his brilliance, he could not seem to figure out that one simple thing.

"I know I had the surgery. I'm just trying to protect us . . . and future us-es. And that's it. Just in case there's a monster in the closet. Instead of, you know—"

"Shirts," Pepper finished as Tony stepped closer to her. With every inch that disappeared between them, her frustration with him melted away.

"You know me so well," Tony said, his voice soft.

"God . . ." Pepper said, almost to herself.

"You finish all my sentences."

Pepper shook her head. This man. This hardheaded, wonderful man. "You should have shirts in your closet."

"Yeah," Tony said wistfully. "You know what there should be? No more surprises. We're going to have a nice dinner tonight." Tony held Pepper's left hand high, the large diamond engagement ring he'd given her shining in the sun. "Show off this Harry Winston." Pepper laughed. He could always make her laugh. "Right? *And* we should have no more surprises. Ever. I should promise you—"

"Yes," Pepper said, being swept away by him once again.

"I will," he said. Tony leaned down into her for a long-overdue kiss. She closed her eyes and the world fell away as it always did when they were together, as though nothing else existed but the two of them and their love.

"Thank you," Tony whispered as she smiled, his lips still pressed against hers.

"Tony Stark."

With a whirl, Tony and Pepper turned to see the surprise. A big surprise. Standing before them was a swirling

124

portal, floating in midair. Inside the portal was the man who had called Tony's name. A man neither of them had ever met before. A man who reminded them that their lives would never be without surprises, despite how many times Tony promised.

The man in the portal spoke. "I'm Doctor Stephen Strange. I need you to come with me."

Seeing Pepper's and Tony's reactions, Strange quickly realized the anxiety-producing effect his rather dramatic entrance had caused. It also dawned on him that, unless he let Tony Stark know he was an ally, this whole situation might get way bloodier. He tried to cut the tension a bit. "Oh, uh. Congratulations on the wedding, by the way."

"I'm sorry. You giving out tickets to something?" Tony asked, his tone short, keeping himself and Pepper at a safe distance.

"We need your help." Strange's voice was measured and serious. He held Tony's gaze as he continued. "Look, it's not overselling it to say that the fate of the universe is at stake."

Tony remained unconvinced. "And who is 'we'?"

Appearing next to Doctor Strange was a man Tony knew *very* well. A man he had sent away, in fact, to avoid causing more destruction. A man he'd lost track of. A friend he had missed and mourned.

Bruce Banner.

"Hey, Tony."

"Bruce," Tony said. His voice soft and worried.

"Pepper," Bruce said, approaching the pair.

"Hi," Pepper said. Her voice was tiny and scared at the haunted look in their dear friend's eyes.

"You okay?" Tony asked, just as Bruce lunged into him for a hug. Tony looked to Pepper in horror as Bruce crumpled into him.

If Tony needed any further convincing, the look on Bruce's face was enough to get him to follow.

Inside the Sanctum Sanctorum a short while later, Tony was receiving a veritable history lesson from Wong.

"At the dawn of the universe there was nothing. Then . . ." Wong wove his hands as golden mystical discs formed around them. Completing the incantation, he thrust his hands forward and an image of five Stones formed out of thin air, floating in space. ". . . the Big Bang sent six elemental crystals hurtling across the virgin universe." The Stones spread out. "These Infinity Stones each control an essential aspect of existence."

Doctor Strange moved forward and pointed to each

Stone individually, naming the aspects. "Space. Reality. Power. Soul. Mind." Strange turned to face Tony, revealing the Eye of Agamotto, which hung around his neck, glowing green. He crossed his arms and the Eye of Agamotto opened, revealing a glowing green Stone inside. "And Time."

Tony felt something gnawing at the edge of his mind, something that had been there for six years. "Tell me his name again."

Bruce stepped forward, the horrors he had witnessed aboard the *Statesman* in his eyes. "Thanos. He's a plague, Tony. He invades planets, he takes what he wants. He wipes out half the population." Bruce's next words confirmed to Tony his darkest suspicions: "He sent Loki. The attack on New York, that's him."

Instantly, ghosts that had chased Tony Stark since he flew a nuclear bomb into space to end the Chitauri invasion, when he witnessed something he shouldn't have in shadow, all became clear. Finally.

"This is it," he whispered. A plan began to form in Tony's mind. "What's our timeline?"

A shrug was all Bruce could offer. "No telling. He has the Power and Space Stones. That already makes him the strongest creature in the whole universe." Bruce's voice softened, as if he couldn't fathom the future. "If he gets his hands on all six Stones, Tony . . ."

Doctor Strange stepped in as Tony began to pace, finally resting his arm on an overlarge metal vase by the destroyed staircase. "He could destroy life on a scale hitherto undreamed of."

Tony gave Strange an incredulous look. He reached behind him to stretch out his hamstrings as he balanced against the vase, keeping his demeanor resolutely casual even in the face of the staggering information he'd just been given. "Did you seriously just say 'hitherto undreamed of'?"

Tony wasn't being cavalier, at least not intentionally. It was just . . . this was how he prepared and processed. If he admitted to himself how dire things were—that if Strange was correct and the fate of the universe was at stake—that meant Pepper's life was at stake. And if Pepper's life was at stake, then he was in serious danger of not being able to think straight. So, in order for him to be of any use to anyone, he had to stay calm. And that meant keeping things light. Even in a situation that was about as unfunny as it could get.

Pointing to the large pot Tony was resting on, Doctor Strange countered, "Are you seriously leaning on the Cauldron of the Cosmos?"

Tony gave the Cauldron the once-over. Despite his massive intellect, being a man of hard science, Tony was unfamiliar with mystical relics.

"Is that what that is?" he asked, almost to himself. Suddenly, the hem of Doctor Strange's Cloak of Levitation rose up and smacked Tony's arm off the Cauldron.

Tony jolted back, surprise crossing his face. He quickly covered. "I'm . . . going to allow that," he said, pointing to the Cloak. He walked away, mind racing as a simple solution popped into his mind. He turned back to Strange, pointing at the necklace around the mystic's neck.

"If Thanos needs all six, why don't we just stick this one down a garbage disposal?"

"No can do." Strange shook his head.

Wong offered an explanation. "We swore an oath to protect the Time Stone with our lives."

Tony let that soak in for a moment . . . then dismissed it. "And I swore off dairy, but then Ben and Jerry's named a flavor after me, so—"

"Stark Raving Hazelnuts," Strange put in.

"Not bad," Tony challenged.

"A bit chalky," Strange corrected, unimpressed.

"A Hunk of Hulk of Burning Fudge is our favorite," Wong said, standing next to Bruce.

"That's a thing?" Bruce asked Wong in disbelief.

Tony cut in, "Whatever. Point is, things change."

Doctor Strange was adamant in his resolve. "Our oath to protect the Time Stone cannot change." He turned his focus to the glowing emerald Eye of Agamotto hanging around his neck. "And this Stone may be the best chance we have against Thanos."

"Yeah, so conversely, it may also be his best chance against us." Tony dug in his heels.

"Well, if we don't do our *jobs*." Strange's voice deepened.

"What is your job exactly? Besides making balloon animals?" Tony shot back.

Strange looked Tony over and let the quiet surround them. Of course, he knew the importance and value of Tony to the world at large. Sure, he'd appreciated all he'd done. But come on. It didn't mean he had to like the guy. Strange was deliberate and pointed as he spoke, his gaze never leaving Tony's.

"Protecting your reality," Strange said without fear or hesitation.

"Okay, guys," Bruce said, addressing them both. "Could we table this discussion right now?" Bruce stepped in between the two arguing men. A slight smile played on Strange's lips when Tony was unable to muster a comeback or have the last word. Bruce pointed to the Time Stone hanging around Strange's neck. "The fact is, we have *this* Stone. We know where it is. Vision is out there somewhere with the Mind Stone and we have to find him now." He had to convince Tony and Strange to stop squabbling with one another so they could come up with a better plan. Having witnessed Thanos firsthand, Bruce paled at the thought of the Titan getting his hands on any more Stones.

"Yeah, that's the thing." Tony scratched his head, a nervous habit and a cue to Bruce that there was something weighing on his mind.

"What do you mean?" Bruce asked, nervous.

Tony tried to break the news as gently as possible. "Two weeks ago Vision turned off his transponder. He's offline."

"What?" Bruce asked, utterly gobsmacked at how Tony could let this happen again.

"Yeah."

"Tony, you lost another super-bot?" Bruce feared the worst, since the last time that happened, Ultron was born. And he was partially responsible for that, a mistake he dreaded occurring again.

Tony quickly sought to assuage his concern. "I didn't lose him. He's more than that. He's *evolving*."

"Who could find Vision then?" Doctor Strange's voice was all business as he tried to maintain focus on the matter at hand. Tony walked away from the group as the answer dawned on him.

Tony cursed under his breath. Who could find Vision? The last person on Earth he wanted to face was the only option he could think of. "Probably Steve Rogers," he muttered.

"Oh, great," Strange said, walking away from Tony.

"Maybe," Tony hedged, unable to look at Bruce. "But . . ." He couldn't. He couldn't say it out loud. The silence expanded.

"Call him," Bruce urged.

"It's not that easy," Tony admitted. Exhaustion, shame, and regret pulsed inside Tony's head. He looked back at Bruce and a tidal wave of emotion suddenly hit him as he realized just how much he'd missed his friend. "God, we haven't caught up in a spell, have we?"

"No," Bruce said, desperate to understand.

Tony shook his head, pushing away all that had happened since he'd last seen Bruce. The good and the bad. Things that weren't his fault and things that very much were. "The Avengers broke up. We're toast."

"Broke up?" Bruce's mind raced. "Like a band? Like the Beatles?"

"Cap and I fell out hard. We're not on speaking terms."

Bruce looked at Tony and realized he still didn't get it. He felt like he was dealing with two kids who'd had a schoolyard fight. The magnitude of what they were facing was way beyond a falling-out between teammates. He had to make Tony understand that the wrath that Thanos

was going to rain down on them would be far more cata-
strophic than some petty fight.

"Tony, listen to me. Thor's gone." Thor's name got
caught in Bruce's throat. The grief and trauma of what
he'd seen was still too raw. "Thanos is *coming*. It doesn't
matter who you're talking to or not."

Tony fought to process what he'd said. Then he
stepped away from the heat of Bruce's gaze and reluctantly took out a flip phone and opened it. A single
contact was listed: Steve Rogers. Tony had yet to use it,
but never could he have imagined that a day like this
would come. As he contemplated calling Cap, a deep
rumbling moved through the Sanctum. The flip phone
still open in his hand, Tony searched the Sanctum for
something that would explain this growing thunderous
sensation. He turned around to see if anyone else was
hearing and feeling the disturbance. Tony looked back to
Doctor Strange. The man's forelock of hair was blowing
ever so gently, back and forth.

"Say, Doc, you wouldn't happen to be moving your
hair, would ya?"

Puzzled by the odd question, Strange looked at the
man. "Not at the moment, no."

All at once, Wong, Doctor Strange, Tony, and Bruce all
gazed up to the source of the breeze: the broken window

high above the foyer. The breeze began to increase in speed slightly. As they noticed this, their senses turned to the sounds of people yelling in the streets, car alarms starting to blare. Bruce backed up, absolute terror on his face. He was the only one of their number who knew exactly what was on the other end of that rumble.

And that meant that he was burdened with understanding just how terrifying the thing outside those doors truly was.

Tony gently opened the front door to the Sanctum, but at his touch it blew wide, crashing open past him with a wave of wind and debris.

Outside, the heroes found dozens of people fleeing what seemed to be a tornado in the middle of the West Village. Dust, papers, and even cars were lifted and flew through the air, obstructing views and adding to the chaos.

Tony stood in the center of it all. And, as the pandemonium raged around him, he steeled himself and got to work, with Strange, Wong, and Bruce following close behind. Tony Stark might not have been the best at explaining prescient dreams to his fiancée, or keeping up the lines of communication with long-lost friends, or taking social cues as to when a situation really did not call for a bit of levity, but saving people?

119

That he was good at.

Tony rushed through the throngs of people as they ran from whatever was at the root of that mysterious rumble.

"You okay?" he asked a felled woman just as a car crashed into a lamppost a little too close for comfort.

"Help her!" Tony barked at Banner and Wong. "Look alive!"

"Go, go! We got it!" Bruce said, waving Tony along. Wong and Banner leaped into action as Tony put on his sunglasses, the display inside illuminated.

"FRIDAY, what am I looking at?" Tony asked his latest computer sidekick.

"Not sure. I'm working on it," FRIDAY answered, her calm Irish lilt belying the absolute anarchy that raged around them.

Tony whipped around to Strange, who was following close behind. "Hey! You might want to put that Time Stone in your back pocket, Doc!"

Strange followed Tony's gaze. His face grew grim. He snapped his arms, and golden discs formed around his wrists.

"Might wanna use it." His voice was dark.

All four men stopped in their tracks when the source of the panic and destruction was revealed. Hovering high above the buildings was a ring-shaped ship spinning vertically. It was not like anything on Earth. Which could only mean one thing.

Time had run out.

118

CHAPTER 3

117

The Queens County Schools yellow bus was filled with loud teens as it crossed the Queensboro Bridge into Manhattan. The students of Midtown School of Science and Technology were buzzing with excitement as they began their field trip. For Peter Parker, however, something else buzzed in him as he felt the hairs on his arm begin to rise. He quickly covered the raised hairs with his other hand and scanned the horizon for impending danger.

This was it. He had to do something. It was like he told Mr. Stark on that first day he came to visit him. That first day when Peter had tried to lie that all those videos of Spider-Man on YouTube were digitally doctored, not real, and definitely *not* him. Of course, Mr. Stark hadn't believed him. He'd seen right through him.

Mr. Stark hadn't visited Peter that day because he thought he was Spider-Man. Mr. Stark had visited Peter that day because he *knew* he was Spider-Man.

In all the weirdness and outside-of-himselfness that went along with becoming Spider-Man, that one conversation with Mr. Stark had made Peter feel . . . okay. Normal, even. Something he never thought he'd feel again.

Peter knew he should feel all these things without needing Mr. Stark's approval. That your friendly neighborhood Spider-Man didn't need the approval of multibillionaire,

Super Hero philanthropists to help out the people on his block. But, whatever. No way. Maybe later. Because right now? Peter wanted Mr. Stark to approve of him more than anything.

Impressing Mr. Stark had become a kind of pastime for Peter in recent months. Because if he could impress Mr. Stark, then he could get called up to the big leagues and finally be one of the Avengers for real, and not just for one battle in Germany that was just against other Avengers, which was so . . . definitely not the big leagues. And if he could get to be one of the Avengers then he could finally—and officially—be of more help. Because it was like what he told Mr. Stark that very first day he came to his house: When you could do the things that Peter could, but you don't, and the bad things happen, they happen *because* of you. Or at least that was how it felt to Peter.

Looking out of the bus window toward Midtown Manhattan, Peter saw the ringlike ship spinning faster and faster. He looked from the ship to the other kids on the bus to see if anyone else saw it. Nothing. Just him. As usual.

Still looking back at the other kids on the bus, Peter reached up to the seat just in front of him where his best friend, Ned, was sitting, blissfully ignorant of any imminent danger. Hurriedly, Peter patted around the proximity of Ned, trying to get his attention. He absentmindedly tapped Ned's upper arm, then his shoulder, then his cheek, then the side of his head. At last, Ned calmly plucked his earbud out and turned to Peter to see what was up.

"Ned, hey. I need you to cause a distraction," Peter said. His voice was urgent, borderline frantic.

Ned looked over Peter's shoulder and saw the ringlike ship himself and immediately understood Peter's urgency.

"Holy crap," Ned said, totally freaked out. Peter waited a few precious few seconds while Ned moved through his initial surprise. Soon enough, Ned jumped into action, providing Peter with the cover he needed. "We're all gonna die! There's a spaceship! Oh, my God!" Ned yelled, racing to the back of the bus to "get a better look" at the alien spaceship that rose high over the Manhattan skyline. The other students quickly gathered around and peered out the side of the bus where Ned was pointing. And just as Peter had asked of his best friend, pandemonium—and a very good distraction—ensued.

Peter dug into his backpack and pulled out his web-shooters, slapping them onto his wrists. Spotting an emergency exit window on the other side of the bus, Peter used his web-shooter to snag the handle. With a quick tug, the latch gave way and the window opened. Peter was out of his seat, across the aisle, and out the window before anyone noticed.

As his fellow classmates continued to freak out at the

sight of the otherworldly vessel, Peter heard the bus driver call for order, adding an exasperated "What's the matter with you kids? You've never seen a spaceship before?"

Now hanging off the side of the bus, Peter quickly covered his face with his Spider-Man mask. Then he reached back into the bus for his backpack and, using his web-shooters, whipped away from the bus over two lanes of traffic and swung down from the Queensboro Bridge, whipping across the East River—on his way to make sure bad things happened a little less when he was around.

Outside the Sanctum Sanctorum, the streets were getting more chaotic by the second. Tony pushed through the brutal winds caused by the ship's presence, ducking behind an open door of an abandoned vehicle. He touched the communicator in his ear and called out to his artificial intelligence system.

"FRIDAY, evac anyone south of Forty-third Street. Notify first responders."

"Will do," came the computerized female voice. Across New York City, FRIDAY changed traffic lights to red; sent emergency notifications to all police, fire, and ambulance departments to assist with the wounded; and closed off all entrances to Southern Manhattan via bridges and tunnels.

Strange walked boldly into the middle of the street right behind Tony. Focused and set on solving at least one of the issues facing them this morning, Strange lifted his arms toward the ship and conjured mystic bands around his wrists. He then produced a spell that encased the offending ship inside its own bubble, finally stopping the rumbling winds once and for all. The papers and detritus floated to the ground as an eerie quiet settled in around them.

Strange lowered his arms, looked over to a reluctantly impressed Tony Stark, and winked. The roaring wind now contained, Tony had to admit that Strange had helped. But that didn't mean he had to acknowledge it. Instead, Tony gave Strange the most chastising side-eye he could muster—hoping that one arrogant showoff disciplining another arrogant showoff for arrogantly showing off wouldn't rip the space-time continuum or anything. Of course, Tony's hard look affected Strange not in the slightest. In a lot of ways, Strange and Stark were more alike than either of them would ever admit.

Joined by Bruce and Wong, the four men began walking toward the ship, just as a beam of energy emanated down and met the ground ten yards in front of the heroes. As it faded, two figures were revealed, one slender, one enormous. Tony sized up the duo as best he could, but found himself completely without answers. Which was almost as annoying as the whole Strange theatrics-wink thing he'd just witnessed.

"Hear me, and rejoice." Ebony Maw's voice cut through

the settling dust as he and Cull Obsidian emerged. "You are about to die at the hands of the Children of Thanos." Cull Obsidian added something vicious sounding in his native tongue, which sounded more like a series of grunts and growls. As Tony grew more and more impatient, Maw continued. "Be thankful that your meaningless lives are now con—"

"I'm sorry, Earth is closed today," Tony interjected flatly. "You better pack it up and get outta here."

Dismissing Tony completely, Ebony Maw turned to Doctor Strange. The Time Stone was practically humming with energy around the Master of the Mystic Arts' neck.

"Stonekeeper," Ebony Maw said. He stared intently at Dr. Strange, who arched an eyebrow at this creature's easy knowledge of him. "Does this chattering animal speak for you?"

"Certainly not," Strange responded, stepping forward. "I speak for myself." Strange conjured the mystic bands around his wrists once more and produced two protective mandalas. "You're trespassing in this city and on this planet." Wong stepped up just behind him, his hands glowing in golden protective mandalas as well.

"He means get lost, Squidward." Tony yelled across the expanse, still smarting from the "chattering animal" thing.

Ebony Maw sighed in exasperation. Sensing Cull's desire for a fight, he waved his thin hand toward the quartet facing them. "He exhausts me." Cull Obsidian answered Maw in his own unintelligible language, bringing his weapon up into battle stance. "Bring me the Stone." At Ebony Maw's words, Cull Obsidian grunted in agreement, and slammed his massive hammer into the New York pavement, cracking it as if it were made of the thinnest sheet of ice.

At the sight of the alien's approach, Tony turned to Bruce, a wry smile on his face. "Banner, you want a piece?"

Bruce winced. "N-n-no, not really," he said sheepishly. "But when do I ever get what I want?"

"That's right," Tony encouraged, patting his friend on the back. Banner shook it off and squeezed his eyes in concentration.

"Okay. Push!" he grunted, summoning "the other guy."

"Been a while. It's good to have you, buddy," Tony said.

"Okay, shhh. Let me just . . . I need to concentrate here for a second." Banner's face contorted and his chest started to swell, taking on a greenish hue.

But then the moment passed. And nothing happened.

Cull Obsidian was getting closer, swinging his hammer at the charred cars parked on the side of the cracked and broken street. Strange shot a look at Stark and Banner, wondering just how much closer they were going to let Cull Obsidian advance before they, you know, defended themselves or, really, did anything at all.

indignation. Tony looked from the rightfully annoyed Strange back to his huffing and puffing—and still very much not a Hulk—friend.

Tony leaned in and muttered, "Dude, you're embarrassing me in front of the wizards."

Blushing, Bruce implored, "I'm sorry. I . . . Either I can't or he won't, or like, I don't—"

"Hey, okay, stand down," Tony said, wrapping a conciliatory arm around Bruce. Stark then lovingly pushed Banner closer to Wong, safely delivering his friend behind Wong's protective mandalas. He motioned to Bruce. "Keep an eye on him. Thank you."

"I have him," Wong said, stepping in front of Bruce protectively.

"Dang it," Banner bit out, confused and frustrated at why this was happening and, more importantly, that it meant he couldn't help his friends against what he knew were the deadliest foes they'd ever faced.

As Cull launched his gigantic body into a run, Tony patted Bruce on the back and stepped forward. He pulled at two cords, one on either side of his vest. Suddenly, his clothing tightened to a black bodysuit, the RT glowing in the center.

As Cull Obsidian approached, Tony, in turn, advanced to meet the behemoth. He tapped the RT, and millions of

"Come on, come on, man!" Bruce grunted, and the transformation again started . . . then quickly reversed. Wong shifted uncomfortably in place, unsure whether to step in or away from whatever it was that Bruce thought he was doing.

"Where's your guy?" Tony asked just as the green hue disappeared from Banner's neck once more, marking the dismal end of any chance at producing the "other guy" and taking on Cull Obsidian with brute strength. Exasperated, and wondering why right now was when he was finding out just how much his friend had changed in the years since they'd seen each other, Tony waited for a response.

Bruce looked embarrassed. "I don't know. We've sorta been having a thing."

Strange and Wong readied themselves for battle as Tony stepped closer to Banner, trying to hide his frustration as he "playfully" punched his shoulder. Stark's pep talk quickly turned into more of a menacing threat as Cull Obsidian stomped ever closer. "It's no time for a thing. *That's* the thing right there," he said, pointing at the oncoming Cull. "Let's go."

"I know that. I just—" Banner strained again, but nothing happened.

Strange turned around and gave Stark a very pointed look. A laser stare that was a lovely combination of disappointment and irritation, bordering on downright repulsed tiny particles spilled out and started to form a sleek version of the Iron Man armor around Tony's body.

Seeing that this was going to be an actual fight, Cull Obsidian raised his hammer as he charged and swung it down hard. Without stopping, Iron Man raised his arm and a triangular shield formed to block the blow. With a mighty clang, hammer hit shield, and stopped the alien's advancement. Cull Obsidian stepped back, dazed by the force of the hit.

Suddenly, two sets of curved metal arcs extended from Iron Man's back, emanating blue light, aimed at Cull Obsidian. The moment they locked into place, missiles launched from each and rocketed straight at the foe, blasting him back straight at Ebony Maw. Maw gave a slight wave and used his telekinesis to swiftly brush the massive Cull Obsidian to the side, barreling his "beloved" sibling into the side of an abandoned car.

"Where'd *that* come from?" Bruce asked, gaping in awe at all of his friend's new toys. Iron Man glanced back, pleased to finally have something to show off in front of Strange and Wong.

"It's nanotech. You like it? A little something I—" Tony was cut off by Ebony Maw, whose powers used the rubble of the street below him to lift Iron Man up, sending him high in the air.

112

Ebony Maw had one focus. One job. To get the Time Stone and bring it to Thanos. Everything else was a distraction. With another wave of his hand, Maw sent an uprooted tree flying toward Wong and Banner, looking to get Strange on his own. Wong acted quickly and put up a mystical barrier around them. The tree dissolved as it hit the shield.

Unable to ensure Bruce's continued safety, Strange realized he had to get Banner as far away from the battle as he could. He turned back to Bruce, whipped his arm in a circle, and opened a portal behind the scientist.

"Doctor Banner," Strange advised, his voice cool and collected. "If the rest of your green friend won't be joining us . . ."

Without finishing his sentence, Strange sent Bruce through the portal . . . where Banner found himself falling from five feet above the ground smack in the middle of Washington Square Park, two blocks away. Bruce landed with an unceremonious thud on the ground. He quickly dodged the back half of a cab that had accidentally flown through the portal behind him, and was now sliced in two as the portal closed behind him.

Back at the site of the battle, Strange and Wong conjured protective mandalas as Maw continued to hurl cars their way. Iron Man zoomed down from the sky, between Wong and Strange, and blasted the oncoming car right back at

Maw. Maw effortlessly split the car in half with his languidly raised hand and his powerful telekinesis. In the precious moments before Maw sent another car flying, Iron Man turned back to Strange with a plan.

"Gotta get that Stone out of here, now," Iron Man said to Strange.

"It stays with me," Strange protested, his voice resolute.

"Exactly, bye." Without hesitation, Iron Man launched off the ground and sped toward Ebony Maw. He was going to bring the fight to him and not just stand there waiting for whatever Maw would throw at them next. Quite literally. If the Time Stone was what Maw really wanted, then Iron Man was going to make the getting of it as annoyingly difficult as possible.

Cull Obsidian, recovered from the blasts, spotted his opponent and swung his hammer. The blunt end disconnected, attached by a chain, and raced at Iron Man. It hit him square in the chest. With a flick of his wrist, Cull twisted the hammer and it hoisted Iron Man from the ground, sending him crashing through a building.

Rubble and debris were everywhere, but the streets were cleared of any civilians as Ebony Maw and Cull Obsidian continued their path of destruction. Cull chased after Iron Man.

His rocket guidance systems knocked offline temporarily by Cull Obsidian's blow, Iron Man careened through the sky and crashed into a tree in Washington Square Park. Bruce ran to his fallen friend.

"Tony, you okay?" he asked. Iron Man's arms and legs were spread out in the miniature crater he had created when he hit the ground. "How we doing? Good? Bad?"

"Really, really good. Really good," Iron Man said sarcastically. His naïve plan to charge Ebony Maw fireworked around in his ringing head. "Do you plan on helping out?"

"I'm trying. He won't come out," Bruce said, still confused and embarrassed by his inadequacy.

Before Iron Man could carry on with whatever existential crisis Bruce was currently embroiled in, Cull Obsidian's hammer sped across Washington Square Park, aimed directly at Bruce.

"Hammer!" Iron Man yelled as he leaped up and pushed Bruce out of the way.

Cull Obsidian's hammer whizzed past the place Bruce Banner's head had been seconds before. With Bruce out of harm's way, Iron Man turned to Cull Obsidian and fired repulsor beams from each gloved hand. Cull blocked the blasts with his shield, sending the energy blasts in different directions.

One of Cull's ricocheting blasts sliced a tree in half and Bruce had to scramble to avoid being squashed. Really? A fallen tree—and not even a big one, by the way—was all it was going to take to end what used to be one of the most feared creatures in the universe? Bruce crawled out from underneath the fallen sapling and clenched his fists in frustration. "Come on, Hulk, what are you doing to me? Come out, come out, come out!" he demanded, slapping his own face as punctuation to every plea.

In a blur, Bruce's face morphed into the Hulk's. Hulk let out a mighty bellow and screamed "NO!" before changing back to Banner. Bruce fell backward, dazed from this ongoing internal mutiny. Lying on his back, surrounded by the branches of the Evil Tree that Almost Killed Him, Bruce screamed in frustration.

"What do you mean, 'no'?" Bruce was at his wit's end. But there was no answer.

The battle between Cull Obsidian and Iron Man raged on in the park. To Tony Stark's amazement, Cull Obsidian's thick hide and alien tech weapon staved off most of his blasts. Iron Man had to think of something quick, because whatever this fight was turning into, even he knew that it wasn't going to be sustainable for long. He'd fought pure brawn before and he'd come out on top. This was different. Iron Man was quickly learning that Cull Obsidian was more than just brute strength.

Cull Obsidian landed a massive blow, sending Iron Man across a small green space. Thankful that it wasn't more concrete, Iron Man came to a stop, sprawled on his stomach, completely vulnerable to the fast-approaching

Cull Obsidian. Disoriented and exhausted, Iron Man was slow to notice the massive hammer descending upon him. But Iron Man both felt the lowering hammer and noticed that its progression toward him had paused at exactly the same moment. Turning, Iron Man saw the person responsible.

Standing over Iron Man was none other than his youngest recruit, Spider-Man. Spider-Man held back Cull Obsidian's lowering hammer as if he were pushing open a kind of sticky window.

"Hey, man." Spider-Man nodded to Cull Obsidian. Turning back to the still-recumbent Iron Man, Spider-Man spoke with only slightly hidden reverence. "What's up, Mr. Stark?"

Peter's voice was as exuberant and light as ever, something Tony both secretly admired and feared. He felt responsible for the kid and, while he was thankful for his help, he felt an immediate burning urge to command Spider-Man to get as far away from this Thanos business as possible. If what Bruce said was true, this battle would be no place for someone as green and unbroken as Peter Parker.

At the same time, Tony knew there was nothing he could do to keep Peter away. Just like Tony, Peter had a code. Save people. Stop bad things. Who was Tony to stand in the way of a man and his code? Even if that man was actually a teenaged boy, and that "code" was more a set of concepts that the kid probably knew how to best articulate through a series of tweets and Instagram updates.

Working rapidly through the scenario at hand, Tony resolved to let Peter fight, but he would also not hesitate to bench him should things get beyond what Peter could handle. He vowed to keep him safe. Whatever that meant for people like Tony and Peter.

"Kid! Where'd you come from?" Iron Man asked, his voice sounding a little too relieved and grateful for his taste.

"A field trip to MoMA," Spider-Man answered just as Cull Obsidian's gigantic hand curled around the kid and hurled him across the park. Spider-Man crashed into a nearby fountain several feet away. He bounced back up, webbing a tree and bounding back into the fight.

"What's this guy's problem, Mr. Stark?" Peter asked as Iron Man circled around Cull, trying to find a weak spot as he blasted the menace.

"Uh, he's from space. He came to steal a necklace from a wizard." If there was a more ridiculous sentence ever uttered, Tony hadn't heard it.

Thwipping and buzzing around Cull, Spider-Man quickly found himself inconveniently trapped inside Cull Obsidian's massive clawlike weapon.

"Hey, hey, hey!" Spider-Man yelled as Cull spun the

captured Super Hero around and around, finally hurtling the boy to places unknown, followed by half a cab just for good measure.

But Spider-Man not only gained control of his own violent and quite unwelcome trajectory, he saw the cab flying toward him and deftly used his web-shooters to lasso the cab and aim it right back at Cull Obsidian. The cab slammed down on top of Cull, finally offering Spidey and Iron Man a second to breathe and try to recuperate before Round Two.

Outside the Sanctum Sanctorum, Doctor Strange and Wong were facing attacks from Ebony Maw. Using his powers, Ebony Maw transformed a pile of bricks into sharpened spikes and sent them hurtling at the mystics. Strange opened a portal in front of him as Wong opened another in front of himself. The sharp spikes flew into Strange's portal and immediately out of Wong's, hurtling right back toward Maw. The creature was shocked to find his own weapons speeding back at his own elongated face. Maw, unused to being challenged in any way, was uncharacteristically slow to act, and that's when one of his own spikes traced a bloody canyon across his grayish, wrinkled visage. His cloyingly impenetrable veneer now gone, Maw targeted a nearby fire hydrant and took out Wong. All of his attention was now back on Strange, and that Time Stone.

But in the one millisecond that Maw was focused on Wong, Doctor Strange swung his hand and conjured a magical whip. He snapped it at Maw and the golden energy weapon encircled the alien. Strange pulled the whip back and forcibly brought Maw toward him.

Maw flew toward Strange, but to Strange's horror, Maw had made the magical whip disappear. Strange braced for impact, only to find himself lifted off the ground. Maw used his telekinesis to slam the mystic against the brick wall of a nearby building. Both now upside down, Maw planted Strange into the wall, covering the mystic's body brick by brick.

"Your powers are quaint. You must be popular with the children," Maw taunted.

With a smug smile, Maw reached for the Eye of Agamotto, eyes glinting at the sight of the Time Stone. But as his hand touched it, he screamed in pain. The necklace had burned itself into the palm of Maw's hand.

"It's a simple spell, but quite unbreakable," said Strange confidently, still partially buried in bricks.

Ebony Maw's dark eyes narrowed to slits and his lip curled in hatred. "Then I'll take it off your corpse." In a fit of frustration, Ebony Maw grabbed Strange by the collar and threw him to the street down below. Strange hit the ground and rolled to safety, finally coming to a kneeling position. His face a mask of intense concentration, Strange

108

crossed his arms and then shot them out to his sides, quickly and efficiently activating the Eye of Agamotto. It opened, revealing the now glowing Time Stone. The glowing green bands encircled the mystic's forearms, but before he could call up its power a deep rumbling came from the ground as dozens of metal pipes and rebar rods shot through the pavement, wrapping around Doctor Strange's body. The Eye of Agamotto closed as a metal pipe twisted around Strange's neck. As the metal tightened, binding him, Strange let out a pained grunt.

Struggling against the bonds, Strange looked to Maw. "You'll find removing a dead man's spell troublesome." Strange's words might have been strong, but his inability to breathe made the uttering of them sound weak and completely declawed. Maw grinned maliciously.

"You'll only wish you were dead." Maw tightened his grip and the metal cage encircling Strange contracted around him, fully incapacitating the mystic. Strange fell to the ground, unconscious and utterly vulnerable to whatever Maw had in store for him. Using his powers of telekinesis, Maw detached the chunk of cement from beneath Strange's body and lifted it into the air. He beckoned the cement, along with Strange, to follow him. Maw was relieved that he'd finally gotten what he came for. Just then, Strange's Cloak of Levitation wormed itself free and, attaching itself to its master, pulled the mystic through the coils.

"No!" Maw was furious at the sight of his prey escaping and zooming away toward Washington Square Park.

In the park, Iron Man was blocking blow after blow from Cull Obsidian with a shield formed from the nanites in his suit. He glanced up to see a barely conscious Doctor Strange fly through the air, guided by the Cloak.

"Kid!" Still fighting the apparently tireless Cull Obsidian, Tony pointed to Strange. "That's the wizard! Get on it!" Tony's voice was ragged.

Peter spun and his jaw dropped at the sight. He was still relatively new to the Super Hero game, but having fought with and against Avengers made him think he'd seen it all. He was wrong. First aliens and a spaceship, now a magic cape carrying a wizard through Washington Square Park. He thwipped his webs and caught the cape like a fisherman hooking a bass.

"On it!" Peter answered. But the Cloak of Levitation had other priorities. Chief among these was getting Strange away from Ebony Maw, who was hot on their trail. So, while the Cloak and Strange flew away from Ebony Maw, Spider-Man chased them both. Once Ebony Maw realized he was being followed, he began hurtling anything he could find back at his pursuer. Spider-Man zigged and zagged, barely dodging an errant billboard that'd been tossed dismissively at him by Maw.

"Not cool!" Peter called out as he doubled his efforts.

As the Cloak of Levitation sped Strange to safety, Maw bent a handful of streetlamps into their path. One of these streetlamps caught the Cloak by the edge, knocking Strange out cold and leaving him open and vulnerable for Maw to intercept. Except before Maw could snatch up Strange—and the Time Stone—Spider-Man used his web-shooters to lasso the mystic himself.

"Gotcha," Spider-Man said to the now-unconscious man. With Strange in tow, Peter swung through the city back toward Iron Man.

But then everything changed in an instant. Doctor Strange was caught in a blue beam that shot down from Ebony Maw's spaceship overhead. Slowly, they began to rise, dust and debris climbing to the heavens with them. Peter had seen enough outer-space movies to know a tractor beam when he saw one.

"Wait!" Spider-Man bellowed. Looking around, he spotted a target: a nearby streetlamp. He fired his webs at it and pulled, the lamp acting as an anchor. The Cloak of Levitation flicked and worried just outside the shaft of light as its helpless master was lifted higher and higher away from New York City. With an effortless flick of his hand, Maw eased the streetlamp from the ground and, with it, Spider-Man followed Strange and the Cloak of Levitation into the blue shaft of light and on toward the awaiting spaceship.

Spider-Man's voice activated the communication radio in his mask. "Uh, Mr. Stark, I'm being beamed up."

In the park, Iron Man was still holding his ground against Cull Obsidian, who was delivering blow after blow. "Hold on, kid!" he managed to grunt.

But Iron Man needed to take his own advice. The brutal truth was that he was losing. He'd lost Spider-Man, he'd lost Strange and the Time Stone, and now he was having trouble just staying in what was turning out to be some kind of pay-per-view heavyweight boxing match with someone who outgunned him in every possible way. He'd been a distraction, all right. But not quite the way he'd planned. Ebony Maw had distracted Iron Man with Cull Obsidian in order to get to Strange and the Time Stone. He'd been had.

His own words to Doctor Strange telling him to get the Time Stone out of there bounced around in his brain, taunting him. Bruce had warned him that this threat was different than anything they'd faced. That Thanos was different. Why hadn't he listened?

106

A piece of Cull Obsidian's armor wrapped around Iron Man's own body armor, jolting and electrifying Tony into submission. As Tony struggled against the iron shackles he could only watch as Cull Obsidian produced a giant metal sword that extended out of his body. Great. Tony's mind filled with exit plans, elaborate schemes, and possible scenarios as his enemy charged into him. In the end, all he could do was try to roll out of the way of the oncoming blow. Instead he was stunned when a portal of energy swirled in the air and enveloped the goliath.

There was a frozen tundra visible for a moment on the other side of the portal before it closed, cleanly cutting off one of Cull's hands.

"Whoa," Bruce said, as Cull's hand rolled over toward him. He kicked it away in disgust.

Bruce and Tony turned to see Wong, mystical golden energy surrounding him, finishing the spell of banishment. Tony leaped up, newly invigorated. He could still fix this. He could still win this. He hadn't lost yet.

"Wong, you're invited to my wedding," Tony said to the mystic as he sped away after all that he'd lost.

Spider-Man and Doctor Strange were still on the trajectory to the spaceship, which had begun to take off. Tony cursed silently. Ebony Maw must have boarded the ship and started piloting it to Thanos, taking Doctor Strange and the Time Stone with him. His stomach dropped even more when he realized that the other cargo Maw had in his tractor beam wouldn't be able to survive for that long in space.

If Tony didn't act quickly, Peter Parker would die. And it would be all his fault.

PART TWO

104

100

99

CHAPTER 4

With the telescopic vision in his visor, Iron Man saw that Peter Parker had managed to climb up his web and cling to the ship. Doing a fast calculation, he determined Peter had exactly 8.6 seconds to live before the spaceship broke the atmosphere, cutting off his air supply.

"Give me a little juice, FRIDAY," he ordered, and immediately personal rockets unfolded from his suit and boots, propelling him with a *BOOM* into the air.

Trying not to panic, Tony barked, "Unlock 17-A."

FRIDAY complied with the order, and miles away, in the former Avengers headquarters, a storage bay marked 17-A opened. A pod sped out faster than sound, its target locked on Spider-Man.

In the meantime, Peter was getting tired, cold, and light-headed from lack of air. His ears were ringing, which was why he thought Iron Man was crazy when he heard him next.

"Pete, you gotta let go. I'm gonna catch you," Tony said, focused and urgent.

"But you said save the wizard!" Peter yelled into the thinning atmosphere. It was difficult to talk. Desperate and panicking, he pulled off his mask. "I can't breathe," he gasped, still holding on to the spaceship with one hand.

"We're too high up. You're running out of air," Tony said, speeding closer and closer to Peter. Even through

97

With the telescopic vision in his visor, Iron Man saw that Peter Parker had managed to climb up his web and cling to the ship. Doing a fast calculation, he determined Peter had exactly 8.6 seconds to live before the spaceship broke the atmosphere, cutting off his air supply.

"Give me a little juice, FRIDAY," he ordered, and immediately personal rockets unfolded from his suit and boots, propelling him with a *BOOM* into the air.

Trying not to panic, Tony barked, "Unlock 17-A."

FRIDAY complied with the order, and miles away, in the former Avengers headquarters, a storage bay marked 17-A opened. A pod sped out faster than sound, its target locked on Spider-Man.

In the meantime, Peter was getting tired, cold, and light-headed from lack of air. His ears were ringing, which was why he thought Iron Man was crazy when he heard him next.

"Pete, you gotta let go. I'm gonna catch you," Tony said, focused and urgent.

"But you said save the wizard!" Peter yelled into the thinning atmosphere. It was difficult to talk. Desperate and panicking, he pulled off his mask. "I can't breathe," he gasped, still holding on to the spaceship with one hand.

"We're too high up. You're running out of air," Tony said, speeding closer and closer to Peter. Even through

97

Tony's fear at what was about to happen, he turned to logic and explanation, his own particular way of attempting to keep Peter calm. What he actually wanted to say was that he was scared and worried. And Tony was scared and worried because he was quickly realizing that, despite his better judgment, he cared for the boy. Felt responsible for him. And those feelings were much more difficult to communicate than the science and facts about what happens to a human being when they fly too high without the proper gear.

"Yeah, that makes sense," Peter said, and Tony's heart broke. Even hanging off the side of a spaceship hurtling into space, seconds from dying, Peter Parker was still just as open and trusting as he'd always been.

After Peter uttered that final sentence, he promptly fell off the ship and slipped down into Earth's atmosphere. Tony was too far away to catch him, but the object from 17-A was right on time. Slamming into Peter's back, it began to form a metallic-like suit that looked like a modified version of his own.

Tony had designed a suit for Spider-Man.

The suit fully formed around Peter, mask included. Spider-Man bounced off the circular ship . . . and stuck like a magnet. Well, more like a spider, Peter thought, as oxygen from the internal systems filled his lungs and his faculties returned to him.

"Whoa! Mr. Stark, it smells like new car in here!"

Relieved, Tony smiled as Peter stood tall in the center of the spaceship's ringlike hull, all decked out in his brand-new Iron Spider Armor. And then it was time for Tony to do what he should have done when Peter had first surfaced in Washington Square Park.

"Happy trails, kid. FRIDAY, send him home," Tony said.

"Yep," FRIDAY answered. Before Peter could ask what Tony had meant, a parachute designed to take him gently through the Earth's atmosphere without burning unfolded behind him, pulling him off the craft.

"Oh come *on!*" Spider-Man yelped as he was whipped away from the spaceship and Thanos and danger and all of Tony's complicated feelings around caring for this kid way too much to focus on the task at hand.

With Spider-Man safely earthbound, Iron Man attached himself to the ship and began using lasers from his gauntlet to cut into the hull. A piece flew out and Tony hoisted himself in.

"Boss, incoming call from Miss Potts," FRIDAY announced just as Tony flew inside Ebony Maw's spaceship. Tony's face fell as Pepper's worried voice crackled through.

"Tony? Oh, my God. Are you all right? What's going on?"

The scene around Tony was like nothing he had seen before. Yet, it was strangely familiar, as were all things Thanos. Pressing a button, Tony activated his boots' stealth mode and he silently began to examine the invading ship.

"Yeah, I'm fine. I just think, uh, we might have to push our eight-thirty dinner res."

"Why?" Pepper's voice was urgent and terrified. It took everything Tony had to keep himself calm and not think back to mere seconds ago when that terror had been his own, directly connected to the possibility of losing Peter Parker.

"Just 'cause I'll probably not make it back for a while." The nanites in Tony's helmet melted away, exposing a face creased in worry as he awaited Pepper's reply. He continued to take in the ship around him.

"Tell me you're not on that ship."

Tony let out an agonized sigh. Pepper got him. She knew him. And even though Pepper had asked the question, both of them knew the answer. He wouldn't be Tony if he weren't on this ship.

"Yeah," he choked out, hating how that one simple word would hurt the only person he'd ever truly loved.

"God, no, please tell me you're not on the ship." Once again, their words entwined and threaded and wrapped around each other's. Even now, they spoke over each other, finishing each other's sentences.

"Honey, I'm sorry. I'm sorry, I don't know what to say, I should—" He wanted to ease her pain, but he knew the only thing that'd do that would be leaving this ship and returning to New York. And he couldn't do that. He wouldn't do that.

"Come back here, Tony. I swear to God. Come back here right now."

"Pep—"

"Come back." Tony listened, frozen.

"Boss, we're losing her. I'm going, too." FRIDAY's voice, and then the call, cut out. Pepper was gone, and he knew that she would be haunted by his absence until he talked to her again . . . saw her again. That meant he had to do what he'd come to do, and fast.

Unknown to Iron Man, it would take more than a parachute to stop Peter Parker from helping less bad things happen. Having detached the chute issued by FRIDAY, Spider-Man was crawling hand over hand on the webbing attached to the vessel.

"Oh, my God," he panted as he managed to flip in through one of the spaceship's emergency doors. "Oh, I shoulda stayed on the bus," Peter muttered, looking down onto Earth far below. The ship's doors closed.

Standing at the controls, Ebony Maw entered coordinates and smiled. He turned, knowing his father would be pleased. The mystic was on his way to Titan, where Thanos would be able to retrieve the Time Stone.

In a flash of light, the circular ship hit hyperspace and vanished into the far reaches of the galaxy.

Miles below, Bruce Banner and Wong stood in the streets of Manhattan, wreckage surrounding them. They watched helplessly as the ship vanished from orbit. Sighing heavily, Wong opened a portal to the Sanctum Sanctorum, stepped through, and began to ascend the crumbling stairs.

"Where are you going?" Bruce asked.

"The Time Stone has been taken," Wong sighed. "The Sanctum remains unguarded." Wong's voice was heavy with responsibility. Bruce noticed it was tinged with sadness. "What will you do?" asked Wong.

Before Bruce could answer, something caught his eye in the rubble: Tony's flip phone. He opened it and, miraculously, it powered on. Steve Rogers remained the only contact in the phone.

Lifting it to his ear, Bruce looked at Wong with a glimmer of hope entering his eye for the first time in years.

"I'm gonna make a call."

CHAPTER 5

ight-years away, a sleek orange-and-silver ship sliced through space, some of Earth's classic hits from the 1970s and 1980s filling the cabin, its highly eclectic crew singing along.

The Guardians' ship.

The crew: The Guardians of the Galaxy.

Nowhere else in the galaxy could you find Star-Lord, a shifty half human raised by pirates; Gamora, a lethal green-skinned warrior raised by Thanos; Mantis, a guileless empath with antennae perched atop her head; Drax, a matter-of-fact muscular alien with intricate tattoos; Groot, a rebellious prepubescent sentient sapling; and Rocket, a foul-mouthed, genetically modified, raccoon-looking creature; all banded together to save the galaxy (and maybe plunder a few leftovers).

"Why are we doing this again?" yawned Rocket, in reference to their current mission.

Still bopping her head to the music, Gamora glanced back at the ship's copilot. "It's a distress signal, Rocket," she reasoned. "Someone could be dying."

Rocket rolled his eyes. "I get that, but why are *we* doing it?"

Peter Quill looked to Gamora. He always looked to Gamora when his virtue was being tested. And not because her moral compass was forged in a life defined by perfect ethical uprightness, but because it was forged amid a life used as a weapon to spread fear, destruction, and bloodshed at the hands of her adoptive father, Thanos. She'd seen every corner of darkness one could imagine, and that she survived with any shred of humanity still intact was a miracle that even Peter Quill could bow down to.

What Gamora and Peter felt for each other—although neither would admit it—went beyond any kind of romantic love, although there was that, too. What they found in each other was their corresponding puzzle piece of brokenness. All of their imperfections, everything they'd been ashamed of, was perfectly cut to fit the other, rendering each one whole at last.

With each other, they belonged. Finally.

But, even with all that, Peter could still, you know, push the boundaries just a little. From time to time. Gamora would understand. (No, she wouldn't.)

"Because we're nice," Peter said, his voice strong and clear. He loved feeling good and proud about his newfound decency. Rocket—less galvanized by whatever this faux-decency was—rolled his eyes, not believing Peter's Good Samaritan act for a second. "And maybe whoever it is will give us a little cheddar cheese for our effort."

"Which isn't the point," Gamora reminded him without turning.

92

"Which isn't the point," Peter repeated, his voice properly grandiose so everyone could hear just how much he truly believed that this wasn't, in fact, the point. And then he continued, but really just as an aside, "I mean, if he doesn't pony up . . ."

"We'll take his ship," Drax said, his voice low and matter-of-fact. Gamora shot him a look.

"Exactly," Rocket said.

"B-b-b-b-bingo!" Peter said emphatically.

"All right!" Gamora looked back at Quill in exasperation. He waved her off as if all of this was just big talk and they weren't actually going to take anyone's ship.

The wordless interaction between the couple took only a few seconds, but the intimacy required to have such unspoken communication had been years in the making. And what they'd built had begun to enter totally new territory. After a lifetime of both Gamora and Quill being burned and disappointed by those who'd promised all of their abuses were just extensions and representations of love, they had finally found someone they trusted, where love didn't have to automatically equate to hurt.

"We are arriving," Mantis said. Her pitch-black eyes widened.

"All right, Guardians, don't forget this might be dangerous, so let's put on our mean faces," Quill announced.

Behind him, Mantis bared her teeth in an imitation of a roar that was more adorable than it was mean or intimidating. The electronic bleeps of a video game cut through the stillness of the ship's cockpit. All eyes turned to Groot, who had grown to the size of a teenager since their encounter with Ego. Apparently, so had his attitude. One leglike branch was slung over the arm of his chair, his attention focused on the handheld game he was playing.

Quill gritted his teeth, a familiar argument brewing. "Groot, put that thing away now. I don't wanna tell you again." A beeping sequence filled the ship as Groot went right along with what he was doing as if Quill hadn't spoken at all. "Groot." Quill's voice became more serious.

Without looking up, Groot made a face and sneered, "I am Groot." The entire crew erupted in shock.

"Whoa!" Quill bellowed.

"Hey! Language!" Rocket scolded.

"Hey!" Gamora warned.

"Wow," said Drax. Groot gave a derisive grunt in response, turning back to his game.

"You got some acorns on you, kid," Quill said, leaning back to get a better look at the rebellious Groot.

"Ever since you got a little sap, you're a total brat." Rocket growled, getting more and more riled up by the second. He lifted himself out of his chair, turned around, and pointed a paw at his impertinent charge. "Now, keep it up and I'm gonna smash that thing to pieces," Rocket threatened.

The argument was cut short by a tiny gasp from Mantis, who pointed to the window of the cockpit. "What happened?"

Through the glass they saw the utter destruction of the *Statesman*. Wreckage, bent metal, lifeless bodies, all floating in deep space. Alone and forgotten. Left to never be discovered.

"Oh my God," Quill whispered in horror. The crew remained in hushed, reverent silence.

Until . . .

"Looks like we're not getting paid," Rocket said, about to turn the ship around.

WHAM!

Something, or rather someone, slammed into the cockpit window. The man's body splayed across the glass. Inside, the Guardians tried to regain their composure, and failed.

"Whoa!" Gamora and Drax exclaimed simultaneously.

"Ew! Wipers, wipers! Get it off!" Rocket exclaimed.

"Oooh!" Mantis squeaked at the sight.

Quill leaned in to look closer, oddly calm. He quickly jumped back as the man's one good eye snapped open.

"How the hell is this dude still alive?"

Quill spoke the question on everyone's mind as they looked at the Asgardian breathing shallowly on the table in their common room. It had taken four of them just to reel him into the Guardians' ship and all of them to put him where he now rested.

"He is not a dude," Drax said reverently. Pointing at Quill: "*You're* a dude." Focusing back on Thor, Drax continued, "This is a *man*. A handsome, muscular man."

"I'm muscular," Quill said, affronted.

"Who are you kidding, Quill? You're one sandwich away from fat," Rocket said with his usual tact.

"Yeah, right," Quill joked, pushing Rocket's words away easily.

"It's true, Quill," Drax said in his standard matter-of-fact tone, and Quill bristled. "You have put on weight."

"What?" Quill was reeling. Drax motioned to his chin and stomach region as Quill looked on in horror. Quill turned to the one person he trusted to tell him the truth no matter what.

"Gamora, do you think I'm . . ." Gamora couldn't look at Quill. Her avoidance was all the confirmation that he needed. He stood open-mouthed as Mantis laid her hands on the sides of Thor's head. She instantly reeled but did not break contact.

"He is anxious . . . angry." Mantis went deeper into

90

Thor's psyche, her eyes widening as she soaked up the full depths of his subconscious emotions. "He feels tremendous loss and guilt."

Drax gaped, still transfixed by the man's physique. "It's like a pirate had a baby with an angel."

"Wow. This is a real wake-up call for me. Okay. I'm gonna get a Bowflex. I'm gonna commit. I'm gonna get some dumbbells," vowed Quill.

"You know you can't eat dumbbells, right?" Rocket mocked as Gamora picked up the man's left arm, scanning its musculature with unadulterated awe.

"It's like his muscles are made of Cotati metal fibers," Gamora said, her voice dripping with admiration.

That was it. Peter Quill had had enough. "Stop massaging his muscles." Gamora "obediently" let Thor's arm drop. Quill turned his attention to Mantis. "Wake him up."

Mantis leaned in and whispered a single word: "Wake."

Chaos erupted as the man lunged up and off the table, roaring. The Guardians all reached for their weapons. Then, the adrenaline rush faded and the man fell forward, bracing himself against the side of the ship.

Breathless and skeptical, the man turned to face the Guardians, glowering. "Who the hell are you guys?"

Gamora knew this day would come. She'd been haunted by it her whole life.

"The entire time I knew Thanos he only ever had one goal. To bring balance to the universe by wiping out half of all life," Gamora began. She stared out the window of the ship as she spoke, unable to look at the people she'd come to care for even though they knew every part of her sordid tale by now. "He used to kill people planet by planet, massacre by massacre."

"Including my own," Drax said, his voice lost in the pain of the past.

Gamora's voice grew dire. "If he gets all six Infinity Stones, he can do it with the snap of his fingers, like this." She punctuated her words with a snap of her own.

"You seem to know a great deal about Thanos," the man, revealed as Thor Odinson, King of Asgard, commented, his tone questioning.

"Gamora is the daughter of Thanos," Drax said helpfully.

Thor's face darkened as he studied her anew. Gamora hung her head. When would she be free of this all-encompassing shame? When would she finally be free of Thanos? Would she ever?

"Your father killed my brother," Thor snarled, standing to confront her.

"Oh, boy." Rocket wasn't sure if he should get between them or move out of the way. He chose to move far away.

Quill, on the other hand, tried to defuse the situation.

"Stepfather, actually." Thor was now within a foot of Gamora, his face no less thunderous than a moment prior. "And she hates him as much as you do." Peter spoke as fast as he could.

Thor came to a stop in front of Gamora. The ship was silent. Gamora looked up at him, her chin high and defiant. She looked him straight in the eye and readied herself for the onslaught.

Thor placed his hand on Gamora's shoulder. "Families can be tough." Gamora eyed his mitt of a hand on her shoulder. "Before my father died, he told me that I had a half sister that he imprisoned in Hell. And then she returned home and stabbed me in the eye." Thor tightened his hold on Gamora's shoulder, much to Quill's displeasure. "So I had to kill her. That's life, though, isn't it? I guess. Goes 'round and 'round and . . . I feel your pain." Quill stepped out from behind Gamora and walked over closer to Thor.

"I feel your pain, as well." Quill stepped in between Thor and Gamora. "Because, I mean, it's not a competition, but I've been through a lot." Gamora rolled her eyes and walked away, not wanting to play into Quill's childish jealousies. Thor loudly slurped the soup that the Guardians had given him as Quill continued to ramble. "My father killed my mother and then I had to kill my father. That was hard. Probably even harder than having to kill a sister.

Plus, I came out with both of my eyes, which was . . ."

Suddenly realizing what was in his hand, Thor held up the utensil, interrupting Quill. "I need a hammer, not a spoon." Thor walked to one of the ship's hanger bays. Inside was a long-range pod, perfect for his needs. He started to mash the buttons on the controls. "How do I open this? Is it some sort of a . . . F-four-digit code, maybe, uh, maybe a birth date or . . . ?"

"What are you doing?" Rocket demanded.

"Taking your pod," Thor answered, as though the question was a silly one.

"No, you're not," Quill said, stepping toward Thor. His voice was lowered and regal, in a sort of mash-up of half-authoritarian tone and half-attempted Asgardian accent. "You will not be taking our pod today, sir."

"Uh . . . Quill, are you making your voice deeper?" Rocket asked.

"No."

"You are. You're imitating the god-man. It's weird."

"No, I'm not."

"He just did it again!" Mantis gasped.

"This is my voice," Quill said in what was definitely not his voice. Thor stepped down with a heavy thud in front of Quill. The two men squared off.

"You mocking me?" Thor asked.

"Are you mocking me?" Quill retorted, mocking him.

"S-stop it. You just, you did it again."

"He's trying to copy me," Quill said, turning to his crew.

"I need you to stop doing that," Thor said, his voice a low growl.

"Enough!" Gamora yelled, in disbelief that she had to discipline two seemingly grown men who should understand how dire their circumstances were.

"He was doing it first," Thor said, needing Gamora to understand how not his fault this whole situation was.

"We need to stop Thanos," Gamora redirected. Thor gave a final glance toward Quill as he continued on toward Gamora. "Which means we need to figure out where he's going next."

"Knowhere." Thor was stating a fact. Knowhere was a deep corner of space known by few. The Guardians were counted among those few.

"He must be going somewhere," Mantis stated obviously.

"No, no. Knowhere? It's a place. We've been there. It sucks," Quill told Mantis as Thor dug through the Guardians' pantry. "Excuse me, that's our food." It was one thing to gift the guy a bowl of soup, but Quill wasn't about to let Thor eat them out of house and ship.

"Not anymore," Thor said, ignoring Quill and examining the parcels.

"Thor, why would he go to Knowhere?" Gamora asked, her voice laced with dread.

"Because for years the Reality Stone has been safely stored there by a man called the Collector."

The Guardians knew the Collector and this information made their stomachs drop.

"If it's with the Collector, then it's not safe. Only an idiot would give that man a Stone," Quill said, growing more and more angry.

"Or a genius," Thor said.

"How do you know he's not going for one of the other Stones?" Gamora asked, her heart racing.

Thor sighed, turned, and faced her.

"There are six Stones out there. Thanos already has the Power Stone because he stole it last week when he decimated Xandar," Thor said, not knowing the impact his words would have.

Gamora, Groot, Rocket, Drax, and Quill exchanged looks. They'd met on Xandar and considered some Xandarians friends. They'd also been the ones to leave the Power Stone in Xandar's capable hands to begin with.

Was this their fault?

Thor continued, his voice grave. "He stole the Space Stone from me when he destroyed my ship and slaughtered half my people." Thor's voice was detached and elsewhere. He still needed time to grieve and process his loss. Now was not that time. He soldiered on. "The Time and Mind Stones are safe on Earth. They're with the Avengers."

The Guardians were confused. Quill asked, "The Avengers?"

"Earth's mightiest heroes." Thor tossed this off casually, as though everyone had heard of them. So busy was he preparing for his journey that he failed to notice not a single Guardian knew what he was talking about.

"Like Kevin Bacon?" Mantis asked, earnestly.

"He may be on the team. I don't know, I haven't been there in a while."

As the only person on the Guardians' ship who actually knew who Kevin Bacon was, Quill furrowed his brow in confusion at the mention that Bacon could possibly be part of this Avengers thing.

Thor continued, "As for the Soul Stone, well, no one's ever seen that. No one even knows where it is." As Thor continued, Gamora turned her gaze to the ground at her feet. The mention of the Soul Stone seemed to make her very nervous. "Therefore, Thanos can't get it. Therefore, he's going to Knowhere."

Thor looked around to make sure everyone was following what was to him plain logic. Unbeknown to him, logic was not the Guardians' strongest suit. *"Hence,"* he said with added inflection, "he'll be getting the Reality Stone."

Thor looked at Gamora, his lesson apparently over. "You're welcome."

Gamora moved to Peter, a plan formulating in her mind. "Then we have to go to Knowhere now," she insisted. She was about to explain the importance of swift action before she was cut off.

"Wrong. Where we have to go is Nidavellir," Thor proclaimed. His order was met with silence, until . . .

"That's a made-up word," Drax accused.

"All words are made up," Thor wisely countered.

"Nidavellir is . . . real? Seriously?" Rocket walked to Thor, his eyes wide and far off, a rare, genuine smile stretching from whisker to whisker. "That place is a legend. They make the most powerful, *horrific* weapons to ever torment the universe." Rocket's voice sounded like a child describing Santa's twisted workshop. It was literally a dream come true to Rocket knowing that Nidavellir existed. He chuckled. Suddenly, eyes coming back into focus, he turned to Thor. "I would very much like to go there, please."

Quill nearly choked at the sound of Rocket saying "please" to anyone, no matter how many weapons a place had.

Gamora shook her head. This had to be a fool's errand.

Thor gave an approving look at Rocket before passing

his judgment to the rest of the crew. "The rabbit is correct, and clearly the smartest among you."

Rocket's chest puffed and he was about to repeat the compliment when one word in particular sunk in. "Rabbit?"

"Only Eitri the Dwarf can make the weapon I need," Thor explained, ignoring Rocket's confused look at being called a rabbit. Instead, he looked to Rocket, gave a slight bow, and placed his fist over his chest as a sign of camaraderie. "I assume you're the captain, sir?"

"You're very perceptive," Rocket answered, confidently and wrongly.

"You seem like a noble leader. Will you join me on my quest to Nidavellir?" Thor asked, looking down at Rocket.

"Let me just ask the captain. Oh, wait a second, that's me!" Rocket grinned from ear to ear.

Thor beamed as well. "Wonderful!" This trip was shaping up to be fortuitous. Until . . .

"Uh, except for that I'm the captain," Quill said, raising his hand in objection as he moved to place himself between Thor and the ship's secondary pod.

"Quiet." Thor's brisk demand was so direct and commanding that it gave even Star-Lord a moment's pause. Which is when Quill noticed the bag Thor had filled with supplies and food for his long journey.

"That's my backpack," Quill said feebly.

"Go sit down," Rocket commanded.

"Look, this is my ship. And I'm not going to . . ." Quill trailed off, trying to remember the name or pronunciation of the place Thor was going. Nothin'. "Wait." Thor turned back to face him. Peter squared his shoulders and tried to be taller as he cleared his throat. "What kind of weapon are we talking about here?"

The answer caught everyone off guard.

"The Thanos-killing kind." Thor's words hung in the common room as everyone absorbed the enormity of such a weapon's possibility.

Recovering first, Quill said, "Don't you think we should all have a weapon like that?"

Thor shot him down. "No. You simply lack the strength to wield them. Your bodies would crumble as your minds collapsed into madness."

"Is it weird that I wanna do it even more now?" Rocket asked.

"Mm, a little bit. Yeah," Thor answered, questioning his choice to bring the rabbit along.

Gamora, having heard enough of dwarves, rabbits, and Thanos-killing weapons, stepped forward as the voice of reason. "If we don't go to Knowhere and Thanos retrieves another Stone, he'll be too powerful to stop." As she addressed the room, her words sunk in. Thor's drove them home.

"He already is." The Asgardian's voice was grave and filled with painful memories.

Rocket, feeling his duty as "captain," barked out a plan. "I got it figured out. We got two ships and a large assortment of morons." Everyone ignored the insult and looked at him to continue. "So, me and Groot will go with the pirate angel here, and the morons will go to Knowhere and try to stop Thanos. Cool?" There were no objections. "Cool."

"So cool," Thor answered.

"For the record, I know that you're only going with him because that's where Thanos isn't," Peter hissed.

Smirking, Rocket raised his voice loud enough for Thor to hear. "You know, you really shouldn't talk that way to your captain, Quill." That was exactly the thing to get under Quill's skin, and Rocket knew it when he saw Peter's face flush red.

Rocket loaded his and Groot's packs into the pod, then looked to find the tree-creature holding his video game too close to the bark of his face, branches nimbly pressing the buttons as the game bleated a new high score.

"Come on, Groot. Put that game down, you'll rot your brain," he admonished.

Groot grunted a rude answer that stunned Rocket. He was about to open his mouth and cut the obnoxious scrawny tree down to size, but there were weapons of torment and destruction to be seen and they needed to begin their journey. All three boarded the pod and were ready to part ways.

Inside the vessel, Thor saluted. "I bid you farewell and good luck, morons."

Only Mantis waved back, the others staring at him, both confused and offended.

Thor smiled at her. "Bye."

With that final word, the pod ejected into space, splitting the team into two distinctly different missions, both of which could determine the fate of the universe. With that thought weighing on the minds of both ships' occupants, the Guardians' ship and Thor's craft sped off in different directions.

84

CHAPTER 6

To the unsuspecting eye, they just looked like any other couple having a boring evening in. She was sipping a cup of tea in bed, and he was gazing out the window as the dark night sky fell across the Scottish landscape just beyond. It was an ordinary evening in every way.

Except for one thing that made it extraordinary: the couple themselves. Wanda Maximoff, better known as the Scarlet Witch, and Vision, Tony Stark's rogue—and possibly evolving—android.

Wanda and Vision had stolen this boring, ordinary evening. They'd protected these forgettable nights with everything they had. They'd fought to sit in bed and drink tea like any other normal couple with a fury and dedication they'd never recognized in themselves before.

Because in this boring room on this forgettable Scottish night, Wanda and Vision were finally free. Free from their endless obligations. Free from the judgment and impossible expectations. Free from the death-defying grind to continually save a world that neither accepted nor welcomed either of them.

There are some in this world who would fight to the death for one seemingly boring evening, so long as they could be together.

A tingling shiver ran through the room as Vision suddenly bent over, clutching his head in pain. He let his fingertips delicately touch the glowing yellow Mind Stone at the center of his forehead.

"Vis?" Wanda asked. Her voice was gentle and worried. "Is it the Stone again?"

Vision's fingers hovered above the Stone curiously. "It's as if it's . . . speaking to me." He sounded confused and a bit fearful. Wanda got out of bed and walked toward him.

"What does it say?" she asked, unsure if she wanted to know the answer.

"I don't . . . I don't know, but something . . ." He trailed off.

She gazed up at him. This face. His face. She knew every inch, every pore, and it broke her heart that he was trying to cover up how worried he was. The tingling Stone rippled through the room once more, and Vision winced. "Hey," she said, and reached up to place her hands on either side of his face. She studied him. He took her hand in his and kissed it, ever fearful that their stolen time together was coming to an end. Whether they liked it or not, the outside world was pushing past their blockades.

Vision closed his eyes as his lips pressed against the palm of her hand. She leaned into him and his eyes eased open, locking on to hers. He led her hand up to the Mind Stone and placed it tenderly atop it. The warmth of her, the feeling of her. It was everything to him. He bent down into her and whispered, "Tell me what you feel." Vision's voice was gentle and ragged. He needed Wanda to use her telekinesis powers to access whatever it was the Mind Stone was trying to say—even though neither of them wanted to remember who they really were outside of this anonymous room.

Wanda looked up at him. The fear and the confusion written on his face. She hated that he was in pain. She hated that they couldn't just have another boring, unencumbered night in. She hated that they couldn't just be . . . normal.

But none of that mattered right now. What mattered right this second was bringing her love a little peace. She pulled her hand away from Vision's head and tiny strands of red energy flickered from her fingers, connected with the Stone, and arced back to her hands.

Wanda honed in on the Mind Stone and dug and searched and hunted for answers. She'd done this so many times, every target's mind laid bare before her. But this was different. She couldn't seem to . . . she couldn't find . . . it . . . she couldn't get past the fog and the blur and the feelings and the warmth and the love and the belonging and home and he was home and she was home with him.

"I just feel *you*," Wanda said. The ease of this confession took her by surprise.

As the rain fell just outside their window, Vis took her face in his hands and kissed her. She became lost in him. Again and again. It didn't worry her that she couldn't read the Mind Stone. It was proof. Something was happening.

Something new and wonderful. Beyond all of the powers and the voices and the chaos in her mind that had hounded her for as long as she could remember . . . she could feel, and beyond that, she could love. She could be felt and be loved in return. She had a chance. They had a chance.

Didn't they?

Dressing slowly, the pair walked outside the inn in search of some fresh air and a hot meal. There was a humming urgency to them as they walked hand in hand down the cobbled streets. The ticking clock of their time together was deafening, and they both knew they had taken way more time than they should have. But it was as if every second became not enough and then the next second only made them hungry for two more, and on and on it went, greedily embezzling time from a universe that acted against them.

"So, there's a ten a.m. to Glasgow, which would give us more time together before you went back," Wanda said, her voice robotic and detached. It was the only way she could get through the next few hours.

"What if I miss that train?" Vision asked. He was clear-spoken, yet sweetly hesitant.

"There's an eleven." Wanda kept herself as unemotional as possible. Her feelings raged just beneath the surface and scared her with their vastness.

"What if I missed all the trains?" Vision stopped and

faced her. He smiled as the thought became more and more real in his head. "What if this time I didn't go back?"

All of the reasons why Vision should go back flooded Wanda's brain. The harsh truth of his wonderful and powerful fair-minded singularity crashed over Wanda. She was being selfish. The world needed Vision more than she did. Although how anyone could need him more than she did was incomprehensible to her.

"But you gave Stark your word." She hated how pragmatic she was being. Why couldn't she just get swept away? Why didn't she believe that she deserved to have this chance at a real life, at happiness?

"I'd rather give it to you." The words were the most serious vow Vision could give her, Wanda realized. Her own heart swelled despite the danger such a decision could mean for them.

"Well, there are people expecting me too, you know? We both made promises." Wanda held back a tidal wave of emotion as the mutinous words spilled from her lips.

"Not to each other. For two years we've stolen these moments, trying to see if this could work, and, I don't know . . . I . . . pers — " Vision took a deep breath, wondering if this was what nervous felt like. "You know what? I'm just gonna speak for myself. I-I-I think—I-I think it . . . It works."

"It works," Wanda agreed, unable to keep from smiling.

"It works," he said again. It felt good to say the words. It felt good to say them again and again. Their smiles were heartbreakingly relieved and scared and wondrous. "Stay. Stay with me," Vision said. His voice was close and enticing.

She looked up at Vision and for the tiniest of moments let herself imagine a world where she stayed. Where they tucked away in their little boring room and drank tea and moved utterly anonymously through this world. The only thing they'd be known for was the great love they felt for each other.

But then they'd have to just stand by and watch as people needlessly suffered because they'd chosen to be so selfish. And however much they loved each other, that burden would begin to erode at the very reasons why they loved each other. And why they'd just begun to actually love themselves.

Wanda painfully slid her gaze away from Vision. Her love for him meant that she couldn't—and wouldn't—keep him all to herself. However much it killed her.

"Or not . . . if I'm overstepping," Vision said, trying to keep things light.

But something else had caught Wanda's eye, through the window of a nearby restaurant. A newscaster was broadcasting footage of the devastation in New York. The hovering ring ships and blurred footage of Ebony Maw and Cull Obsidian made Wanda cover her mouth in horror.

She could barely find her voice enough to ask Vision, "What are they?"

A long sigh preceded Vision's answer. "What the Stone was warning me about," was all he could say.

What flashed on the screen made them both take notice: TONY STARK MISSING!

Vision grabbed Wanda's hand and kissed it, turning away as he did so, readying himself for what lay ahead. "I have to go."

But Wanda refused to let go. "No, Vision. Vision, if that's true, then . . . then maybe going isn't the best idea." Wanda was panicking.

"Wanda, I—Guhhhzz." His eyes widened in shock and pain as he bent over at the waist.

"Vision!" Wanda's red magical energy surrounded her hands like a crackling mist now as she looked in horror at what had become of her love.

A sharp blade was piercing his chest and lifting him three feet from the ground. Vision's human appearance faded as his skin turned red, and his clothes shifted to his green-and-gold caped outfit. Screaming, he was dismissively flung into the middle of the cobbled street.

Behind Vision, Corvus Glaive growled.

Wanda's eyes narrowed.

The glow from the Scarlet Witch's hands grew more

intense and a heightening, glaring shade of red as she moved her hands to cast a spell. She lifted her hands, aimed—and was hit by a bright blue blast before she was able to do anything to save Vision. Wanda's body was launched through a display window on the other side of the street. Proxima Midnight stood, holding a staff buzzing with blue energy arced across the tips on either end.

Vision lay on the ground, paralyzed temporarily, with Corvus Glaive and Proxima Midnight standing above him. Corvus Glaive had taken out the blade and was tapping it against the Mind Stone in Vision's forehead. Although the Stone was far more powerful than the blade, Vision let out a scream, feeling as if the blade was piercing his very brain. Corvus shifted his weight, replaced the blade against the Stone, and tried once more to pry it out.

Before Vision could even cry for help, both foes were sent soaring two blocks away. Vision turned his head and saw the Scarlet Witch, fully powered and fully angry, stepping out of the now broken display window. Wanda moved her hands and the dancing red bolts encircled Vision, lifting him off the ground and away from Corvus and Proxima. Wanda flew off after him and, her magic continuing to hold him aloft, successfully transported them far enough away to see to his wounds. She pulled him into a darkened alley, set him gently on the ground, and started stitching up the gaping hole from the blade with her powers.

79

"The blade. It stopped me from phasing." Usually he could pass through any solid object with a thought.

"Is that even possible?" Wanda asked, focused on his injury.

"It isn't supposed to be-be-b—" Vision momentarily glitched as sparks flew from the hole in his chest. His tone softened. "My systems are failing." Wanda pressed on, unable to accept that this wound or these enemies were anything but completely beatable. She wasn't going to lose Vision. Not like this. Not ever.

She remained easy and undaunted as she stitched, hoping to provide him with the peace that he'd given to her time and time again. As she worked, she was desperate in her compartmentalization. If she believed for one second that she would lose Vision, she . . . she . . . what would be left for her? How would she go on?

No. Absolutely not. He would be fine.

He had to be. He had to be.

Forcing a smile, Vision thought back to just a half hour earlier. "I'm beginning to think we should have stayed in bed," he chuckled to Wanda. The glint in his eye left quickly and he shoved Wanda away just in time. Corvus Glaive pounced onto the exact spot the Scarlet Witch had been kneeling. Now instead of Wanda's peaceful, loving face, Vision saw a creature that wanted him dead crouched above him.

Corvus Glaive grabbed Vision by the neck and sprung high in the air with his taut muscular body. The pair came crashing down against a church a few yards away.

"Vis!" Wanda screamed. She ran into the street and quickly dodged an arc of blue lightning. She had anticipated that Proxima Midnight would be there and listened for her weapon's hum.

Proxima marched toward the smaller woman, her face contorted in rage. Not to be outdone, Wanda sneered back, hands red and ready to fight. Proxima Midnight swung her staff at Wanda, but this woman had been trained by the greatest fighters on Earth. She bent backward at the waist, letting the staff fly over her. As it passed, Wanda unleashed a spell that used the staff's momentum to carry Proxima Midnight ten yards away.

Wanda turned her attention to Corvus and Vision, the latter seriously injured and barely able to fight. Before Wanda could help him, however, her distraction cost her — Proxima Midnight's staff struck the Scarlet Witch in the back, causing her to cry out.

Corvus Glaive growled a compromise. "Give us the Stone and she lives."

Letting out a primal scream of his own, Vision grabbed Corvus by the neck and launched him high into the sky. They careened into a church steeple and pitched onto a far-off roof, before rolling to a painful and exhausting stop. Both leaped up and continued brawling until Vision unleashed a powerful beam of energy that emanated from the Mind Stone. Corvus Glaive had a millisecond to block the brunt of the blast with his blade, sending streams of energy flying across multiple directions in the town center. One beam reflected perfectly and hit Vision in the chest, knocking him back.

Her attention on the fight between Corvus and Vision, Proxima Midnight failed to see Wanda's hands recharge until it was too late. She sent the villainess soaring into a now fully engulfed vehicle blazing on the side of the road. With Proxima momentarily taken care of, Wanda shot to where she could hear Vision's screams. She found Corvus once again huddled over her love, blade pressed violently to the Mind Stone on Vision's forehead. Walking toward him, even Wanda's eyes began to glow.

"Hands off." It wasn't just a warning. Corvus Glaive was lifted a dozen feet in the air and sent flying. Wanda picked up Vision and then lifted herself and him up high into the air. But not high enough. From the ground, Proxima aimed her staff at the couple, sending a blue blast at them. It was a direct hit, and Wanda and Vision fell through the roof of a nearby train shed.

They landed with agonizing force, sliding and rolling along the shed's ground floor. Wanda bent over Vision and tried to lift him. "Come on, come on. Come on. You gotta get up." But he didn't move. Undeterred, Wanda insisted. "You gotta get up. Come on. Hey, we have to go. Okay." Wanda was on autopilot. Every inch of her body was broken in some new and horrific way, but she felt no pain. She had one goal. To get Vision to safety. And nothing was going to get between her and achieving that.

The slightest smile crossed Vision's lips as he reached up and touched her face. He loved her, and because he loved her he needed her to get as far away from him as possible. She didn't understand how badly he needed her to live. She'd given him more life than he had any right to have. She'd loved him. Truly loved him. Something he never thought he'd be able to experience. How could she ever truly grasp what she'd given him? "Please. Please leave."

Wanda leaned in. "You asked me to stay. I'm staying," she said, ferocious and intense.

"Please" was all Vision could say before Proxima Midnight and Corvus Glaive broke through the roof one by one. They walked to the fallen couple, ready to finish the fight for good.

Wanda and Vis would die together. Right here. Tonight. Because if only one of them died, there was no point in the other living.

Wanda stood and faced both of her opponents as an express train passed through the station just behind her.

77

The town was too small for it to stop, but between the cars, Wanda swore she saw . . . something. Someone? Proxima Midnight followed her look. As the train passed, it was obvious a figure stood in the shadows.

Proxima threw her spear at the figure. The man caught it and stepped into view. Hair mussed slightly, a blond beard, and a black tactical suit with a familiar star pattern sewn onto the chest made Wanda audibly sigh in relief.

Captain America had arrived.

Steve Rogers's presence rippled through the abandoned rail yard. He stood unmoving and completely composed in front of Proxima and Corvus, who were so confident moments before and were now backing away hesitantly from their prey.

And because their attention was focused solely on Captain America, neither Corvus nor Proxima noticed Sam Wilson, also known as the Falcon, swoop in from just behind them.

Sam kicked Proxima across the rail yard and all the way through a nearby storefront. As Corvus reeled, Sam circled back around and fired four missiles at the slender child of Thanos. One of Sam's errant missiles exploded against a wall, briefly backlighting Black Widow as boldly she ran, directly at Corvus Glaive.

Steve threw Proxima's staff through the air to Black

Widow's outstretched hand. Natasha caught it without missing a beat, slid under Corvus's slicing blade, and swung. The staff and Corvus's blade sparked as they clashed together.

The two sparred, staff versus spear, for a few moments. Having never faced her before, Corvus didn't realize until it was too late that Black Widow was merely testing him to discover his weak spot.

With no warning, Natasha twisted quickly, dropping to a crouched position, and jammed Proxima's staff deep into Corvus's side. Corvus dropped his staff and let out a howl as Natasha drove the spear in deeper. She wanted to make sure he wasn't going to reenter the fight.

Feeling the staff shake in her hand, Black Widow let it go quickly, just in time for it to fly through the air, summoned by Proxima Midnight.

Somersaulting into the fray, Cap scooped up Corvus's staff and blocked Proxima's deadly lunge at Natasha. As Cap and Natasha battled Proxima, Sam saw his opening and swooped back in to kick her once again across the rail yard, and she landed just feet from her fallen partner.

Cap and Natasha stood over the wounded and incapacitated pair. Sam landed next to them and drew both of his weapons.

"Get up," came Proxima's deep, rumbling voice.

Corvus answered weakly, "I can't."

"We don't want to kill you, but we will," Black Widow said, her voice an icy rasp.

"You'll never get the chance again," Proxima warned. Her voice seemed to echo. The trio watched in stunned silence as a blue blaze shone around Proxima and Corvus, lifting them through the rail yard and into the waiting spaceship overhead, pulling Corvus's spear right out of Cap's hand.

As the spaceship flew away, the trio refocused on what mattered: Wanda and Vis.

"Can you stand?" Sam asked Vision, then offered a hand. With one arm around Sam and the other tight around Wanda, Vision finally struggled to a somewhat upright position. Cap and Natasha stood in front of him, taking in the glitching and severely wounded android.

"Thank you, Captain," Vision said.

Weary himself, Captain America's face was stoic as he accepted Vision's thanks. His eyes slid up to the Mind Stone firmly lodged in Vision's forehead, a reminder that this wasn't just some accidental reunion of old friends. Whatever the last two years had been—a break, a hiatus—they were officially coming to an end. Cap knew his next words would put into motion a series of events that not even he could control.

"Let's get you on the jet," Cap said, trying to keep his voice deceptively light.

Moments later, Cap, Falcon, Black Widow, Scarlet Witch, and Vision—all outlaws thanks to the Sokovia Accords—were aboard a Quinjet, taking off from the Scottish village where Wanda and Vision had found their calm and peace.

"Now, I thought we had a deal. Stay close, check in, don't take any chances," Black Widow said, exhaustion and mild frustration weighing down each of her words.

"I'm sorry. We just wanted time," Wanda said, settling in next to Vision.

Her words hit Steve as he stood in the center of the Quinjet. Time. For someone who'd had more than his share of time on Earth, he never seemed to have any for himself. He understood exactly why Wanda and Vis would want to steal a little of the precious commodity.

"Where to, Cap?" Sam asked, sitting at the Quinjet's controls. The words snapped Steve out of whatever momentary elsewhereness he'd allowed himself to get lost in.

Steve looked at Vision and Scarlet Witch. They had grown so much over the past two years. Individually and together. But they had no idea what he knew about what was coming for them. Or how much everyone in that Quinjet would need each other. His decision was an easy one to make. His voice was clear and resolute as he spoke.

"Home."

CHAPTER 7

"Shhh," a mother said, gently covering her whimpering child's mouth. "We'll be safe. We'll be safe."

The Zehobereian woman brushed her daughter's scarlet hair back from her emerald-green forehead. This was a special child. Surely the invaders, visible through the wooden slats of the hut in which they hid, would recognize that and spare them.

Outside, the screams of the Zehobereians grew louder as life after life was cut short by blaster fire from ruthless soldiers who served the feared Thanos. The girl's mother never imagined the Titan would target her peaceful planet, as he had so many others, to the point where his name even whispered on the wind caused a bone-chilling fear. The little girl screamed.

"Shhh, Gamora," her mother desperately whispered. But it was too late.

With a massive crash, the shed doors splintered inward from a soldier's heavy kick. The young girl screamed as she was ripped from her mother's arms. The Zehobereian people were divided into two groups with a wide path between them. Ringed ships hovered above. An insectoid army pushed and shoved, forcibly keeping the two groups apart. The young girl was carried to the opposite side of where her mother stood, the older woman weeping both in sadness knowing she wouldn't get to see her child grow up, but also in joy, knowing her daughter would live.

"Mother!" Gamora cried, as she was being violently pulled farther and farther away.

"Zehobereians," spoke the melodic voice of Ebony Maw as he strolled down the path that divided the population in half. "Choose a side. One side is a revelation, the other an honor known only to a few."

The daughter ran up and down the sides, searching. "Where's my mother? Mother!" the little girl demanded, courageous even in the face of potential death. She ran past a guard, deftly dodging him, and directly to the man she knew was responsible. The man who wore the helmet and armor of a commander. The man whose lavender-hued skin was tougher than those of most animals she'd ever seen hunted.

Thanos bent down. "What's wrong, little one?"

The girl put her fists on her hips and dared to glare at Thanos. "My mother. Where is my mother?"

The Titan crouched down, bending so they could speak face-to-face. "What's your name?"

"Gamora," the girl spat out, her tone challenging.

"You're quite the fighter, Gamora." He extended his hand to her. "Come. Let me help you."

She extended her hand, letting her tiny fingers wrap

around the Titan's index finger. The two walked away from the parted crowds to an open-air hut, where Thanos knelt.

Thanos produced a small red handle and showed it to Gamora. "Look. Pretty, isn't it?" Gamora shrugged. Thanos touched a button and twin blades extended from either side. At that, Gamora's eyes widened. He balanced the blade, his index finger placed strategically below a large red gem at the ornate center of the blade's hilt.

"Perfectly balanced, as things should be," Thanos instructed. "Too much to one side or the other . . ." As he spoke, he let the blade wobble, nearly falling, before centering it once again. He held it out to his new protégé. "Here, you try." Gamora reached for the blade, which looked much larger poised on her tiny hand. She tried to balance the blade just as Thanos had.

Behind them Ebony Maw had finished his march between the Zehobereians, having successfully divided them into two equal groups.

"Now," Maw proclaimed, "go in peace to meet your maker."

From one side of the Zehobereians, Thanos's soldiers stepped forward and opened fire. Both sides screamed. Just as Gamora was about to turn her head, Thanos directed her attention back to the balancing blade. He knew which side her mother was on and wanted to spare Gamora the sight.

"Concentrate," he said, as she started to gain control of the blade, the hilt in the center of her finger, neither blade moving. Thanos smiled. "There. You've got it."

And with that, Thanos knew he had a new daughter as well. One who would grow up to be his most precious child of all.

Holding the very same blade in her hand so many years later, Gamora stared out as the Guardians' ship approached Knowhere. Her thoughts were interrupted by the familiar footsteps of Peter Quill. Star-Lord was outfitted with extra weapons for the attack on Thanos. Lifting a grenade belt, he was about to question her when she held up her hand.

"Gamora. Do you know if these grenades are the 'blow-off-your-junk' kind or the gas kind? Because I was thinking about hanging a couple on my belt right here, but I don't want to if they're the—"

"I need to ask a favor," Gamora cut in.

"Yeah, sure." Quill shrugged.

Gamora sighed as though the weight of the universe rested on her shoulders. "One way or another, the path that we're on leads to Thanos." Gamora stood.

"Which is what the grenades are for," Quill joked, throwing one high into the air and catching it. Gamora looked over at him, her eyes serious and pleading. She needed him. Quill's face immediately softened.

"I'm sorry. What's the . . . what's the favor?" he asked, his voice a somber whisper. Gamora turned away from him.

"If things go wrong . . ." Quill listened, his brow furrowing with each wrenching word Gamora spoke. "If Thanos gets me." The words caught in her throat. She turned to look at him. Her eyes pleading and urgent. "I want you to promise me . . ." Her voice softened to a hoarse whisper. "You'll kill me."

"What?" Quill just stared at Gamora. Waiting. Hoping that he'd heard wrong. That she didn't mean he should actually—

"I know something he doesn't." Gamora turned away from him, unable to continue to watch as the true weight of her request began to sink in. "And if he finds it out, the entire universe could be at risk."

"What do you know?" Quill asked, serious.

"If I tell you, you'd know, too." Gamora was matter-of-fact. Quill understood immediately what she was doing. He stepped closer to her.

"If it's so important . . ." He trailed off as he reached out to her, his fingers curling around her arm. His touch softened her, and she finally turned to him. "Shouldn't I?"

"Only if you wanna die." Her voice was an agonized whisper.

"Why does somebody always have to die in this scenario?" protested Quill. She stepped closer to him.

"Just trust me. And . . . possibly kill me," she said, swallowing. Gamora could see Quill putting back up his defenses. For him, there was always a plan—or at least a percentage of a plan—that would keep him and his people safe. What Gamora was proposing sounded way too final. And Quill wasn't ready to admit that things had already become as dire as Gamora was making them out to be.

He needed to pull her out of this. He needed to make her see that things were going to be okay and that they'd survive this, just as they'd survived everything else. He needed her to stop with all this talk about somebody dying and get her back to thinking about the long and economically abundant future that awaited their perfect little dysfunctional family of misfits.

"I mean, I'd like to. I really would. But you—"

Gamora put her hand over Quill's mouth. She needed to stop him before he retreated completely back into his safe little world, where he took nothing seriously and any real emotion was for suckers.

"Swear to me." Gamora's eyes locked on to his. "Swear to me on your mother," she said, bringing Quill to the one place he'd be forced to keep his word. She pulled her hand away from his mouth as Quill's eyes told her that he finally understood. It took a long time for him to answer. Up until this point, he'd always been able to talk himself out of any situation, but right now he was at an absolute loss for words.

"Okay." Gamora looked up at him. And he nodded. He got it. He finally got it. "Okay," he repeated. No jokes. One simple word.

The silence expanded as Gamora looked up at him, tears falling. Quill reached across and wiped away her streams of tears with the back of his hand. She let him comfort her. She let herself be loved by someone. So loved that he would save her from the one thing she couldn't conquer on her own. She leaned into him and kissed him. Wordlessly thanking him for loving her enough to find the courage to kill her, if it came to that.

As Quill and Gamora got lost in each other, a loud crunch rippled through the room. They looked across the room to find Drax, standing in the shadows, eating a bag of zarg-nuts.

"Dude, how long have you been standing there?" Quill asked, replaying all that Gamora and he had talked about, not to mention their passionate kiss.

"An hour," Drax answered.

"An hour?" Quill echoed in disbelief.

"Are you serious?" Gamora asked.

"I've mastered the ability of standing so incredibly still

that I've become invisible to the eye. Watch." Drax's voice was mysterious and serious as he pulled a zarg-nut from the bag and lifted it to his mouth. Fully visible. To everyone. Not invisible at all.

"You . . . you're eating a zarg-nut." Quill couldn't stand whatever Drax was doing for one more second.

"But my movement was so slow that it's imperceptible—"

"No." Both Quill and Gamora shook their heads.

"I'm sure I'm invisible." Drax held firm.

"Hi, Drax!" Mantis said, walking into the room.

"Dang it." Drax crumpled the zarg-nut bag and huffed out of the room.

Knowhere held no one, it seemed.

"This place looks deserted," Quill said as their ship flew overhead, scanning the abandoned, empty world.

"I'm reading movement in the third quadrant," Drax offered.

Gamora tried to prepare herself as best she could. Would Thanos be lying in wait? Had he been here already? She'd always known—deep down and with every possible scenario that she had braced herself for—that it'd be just a matter of time before she would come face-to-face with Thanos. Every path led directly to him. It always had. Her face fell as the reality of all this washed over her.

"Yep. I'm picking that up, too," said Quill. "Let's put it

down right here." He piloted the Guardians' ship to a safe landing amid the remnants of the planet.

They reached the former site of the Collector's museum, which was now just a shell of its former self. The Guardians crept through the ransacked cavernous space of oddities and riches that had been gathered throughout the ages and placed on display there. They came to a sudden stop when they heard the low grumbling voice of Thanos ordering Tanleer Tivan, the Collector, to surrender the Stone. "Everyone in the galaxy knows you'd sell your own brother if you thought it would add even the slightest trinket to your pathetic collection."

Gamora steeled herself as Thanos's voice echoed throughout the abandoned museum.

Quill held up a fist, signaling to the rest of the Guardians to freeze. One by one, they walked past him, each completely ignoring their captain. With a sigh, Quill caught up with his insubordinate crew as they took in the scene playing out before them. The Collector was on his back and lying on the floor, bloodied and begging for his life. Thanos stood over him, unarmored and impatient.

"I know you have the Reality Stone, Tivan. Giving it to me will spare you a great deal of suffering." Thanos stepped forward, placing a heavy foot in the middle of the Collector's chest.

"I told you. I sold it. Why would I lie?" The Collector's

words were ragged and choking, the weight of Thanos's foot slowly wringing out every last breath.

"I imagine it's like breathing for you." Thanos looked down at the squirming Collector with disdain.

"Like suicide." A haunting glint shimmered in the Collector's wild eyes.

"You do understand." A smile curled across Thanos's face. "Not even you would surrender something so precious."

"I didn't know what it was." The Collector's words were pained and pleading.

"Then you're more of a fool than I took you for." Thanos looked away from his prey, seeming to contemplate whether he believed this version of the truth.

"It's him," Drax fumed, watching from the sidelines.

"Last chance, charlatan. Where's the Stone?" Thanos pressed his foot into the Collector's chest.

Drax inhaled a deep breath. "Today—"

"Drax. Drax—" Quill tried to get Drax's attention before he did something stupid, like the last time they were on Knowhere and he decided to take on Ronan the Accuser all by himself. It didn't work out then and was going to work out even worse now.

But Drax was past the point of listening to reason. "He pays for the deaths of my wife and daughter."

"Drax, wait." Drax unsheathed his knife as Quill

desperately whispered warnings at him. "Not yet, not yet, not yet." Quill sped around, trying to cut the fast-moving Drax off at the pass. "Drax. Drax, Drax, Drax. Listen to me. He doesn't have the Stone yet. If we get it, then we can stop him. We have to get the Stone first."

"No. No. For Ovette. For Camaria." Drax lunged for Thanos, but Mantis had crept up behind him, placing her hand on him and whispering "Sleep" right at the last moment. The large man fell like a stone.

The thud of Drax's fall echoed around the museum and, as Thanos scanned the area, the remaining Guardians ducked for cover.

Thanos lifted his foot off the Collector's chest and tossed him into one of his own display cases. Looking around for the source of the loud thud, Thanos began striding in their direction.

"Okay," Quill hissed. "Gamora, Mantis, you go right . . ." Gamora began to charge in from the left, swords raised, leaping to get higher ground. "The *other* right."

Gamora caught Thanos by surprise, but the large Titan barely swatted away one of the blades before she could deliver a killing blow. Another strike, another deflection. Father and daughter were grunting with every parry and jab, focused only on the battle at hand. A battle that could save the universe, or destroy it.

As Gamora swung a blade at Thanos's head, the

person she once called "Father" caught the sword between his hands and snapped it in half. Not stopping, Gamora angled her body and thrust, the sword finding its mark. She plunged it into Thanos's neck.

The foe's eyes widened in shock, grabbing the blade to pull it free, but Gamora had one last trick in store.

From her boot, Gamora revealed the perfectly balanced hilt: the first gift Thanos ever gave her. She popped both blades out and let it dance briefly on her finger before . . . *thunk!* She plunged the balanced blade into Thanos's chest, restoring order to the universe.

"Why?" Thanos croaked. He fell to his knees before falling onto his back against a twisted and destroyed display case. Gamora began to cry as he reached his hand out to her. "Why you, daughter?" Gamora collapsed into sobs as she watched his outstretched hand fall lifelessly to the ground beneath it. The Collector watched in disbelief from inside his display case.

"That was quick," Quill said to a now awakened Drax, both still on the sidelines. The Collector started clapping.

"Magnificent! Magnificent! Magnificent!" He cheered as Gamora continued to sob.

"Is that sadness I sense in you, daughter?"

Gamora looked down, but Thanos's body was disappearing. His voice, however, echoed through all of Knowhere.

"In my heart, I knew you still cared. But no one really knows for sure."

Around them, Knowhere changed. The Collector disappeared from the case he was held in. Jars were shattered, priceless artifacts smashed. Worse, everything was in flames.

All of Knowhere burned around them, destroyed by Thanos's army.

The madman's voice growled once more. "Reality is often disappointing."

A slight gust of wind sucked past them as a slice of the world opened a void in the fabric of reality itself. Thanos, holding up the Infinity Gauntlet, revealed the three Stones now in his possession, including the glowing red Reality Stone.

"That is, it was." He grinned wickedly. "Now, reality can be whatever I want."

As the actuality of their surroundings was fully revealed to the Guardians, Gamora paled. "You knew I'd come."

"I counted on it," he said plainly. "There's something we need to discuss, little one." Gamora looked up at Thanos and then lunged forward for her sword. But Thanos was too quick. And in an instant, he scooped her high up into the air as the sword clattered to the floor.

Drax, his mortal enemy and killer of his family in sight, roared at the Titan. "Thanos!"

As he lunged forward, both knives high in the air, Drax began to change. Lit by the glow of the Reality Stone on the Infinity Gauntlet, Drax's body was spotlighted as it began to cube and fall apart like myriad clay building blocks.

Gamora saw Thanos turn to Mantis, a wicked smile on his face. "No!"

But she was too late. Mantis's body unspooled like ribbons, twisting and springing around.

Thanos gripped his daughter and pulled her in tightly. No tricks this time.

"Let her go, Grimace!" bellowed Quill, blaster raised. Thanos looked at Quill with a bemused tilt of the head.

"Peter," Gamora begged, tight in Thanos's clutches.

"I told you to go right," Quill said, signaling that he had no intention of keeping his promise.

"Now? Really?" Gamora asked, her voice choking.

"You let her go!" Quill yelled.

"Ah. The boyfriend." Thanos sounded underwhelmed.

Peter's eyes were aflame with rage. "Like to think of myself more as a Titan-killing, long-term booty call." His fingers tightened around his blaster. "Let. Her. Go." He spat out every word.

67

"Peter," Gamora pleaded.

"I'm gonna blow that chin right off your face—" But Quill was interrupted by Gamora, once again calmly calling his name.

"Peter. Not him." She was in tears, but her breathing was finally steadying. Quill looked at her and the moment expanded as he kept his blaster safely trained on Thanos and not Gamora. His mind reeled, looking for another way out. Any other way out. Gamora sensed his hesitation.

"You promised," she implored him. She choked out her plea once more. "You promised."

With every ounce of control he had, Quill lowered his blaster so it pointed directly at the love of his life. Gamora breathed in a gasp of relief and closed her eyes.

"Oh, daughter. You expect too much from him." Thanos zeroed in on Quill. "She's asked, hasn't she?" Gamora looked at Peter, becoming more and more resigned. "Do it." Thanos egged him on as the tears began to well up in Peter's eyes. Running out of patience, Thanos stepped forward, shoving Gamora right into the end of Quill's blaster. "Do it!" he bellowed.

Peter's voice cracked. There was no other way and he knew it. "I told you to go right. . . ."

"I love you more than anything." Looking directly in Peter Quill's eyes, Gamora said the words for the first time, and probably the last.

Peter didn't hesitate. "I love you too."

The pair closed their eyes, not wanting to look as they fulfilled their pact. Gamora braced herself, heard Peter squeeze the trigger, and exhaled as she felt . . .

. . . bubbles? Dozens of bubbles rose from the barrel of Peter's blaster. The red glow of the Reality Stone made them glimmer like ethereal rubies.

"I like him," Thanos chuckled.

Before Peter and Gamora could realize what was happening, a cloud of black smoke enveloped Thanos and his captive daughter, teleporting them far away.

Drax and Mantis began to regain their normal forms, but Peter, holding Gamora's broken sword, felt in his gut that nothing would ever be normal again.

PART THREE

CHAPTER 8

Emotions were running high in the Avengers Headquarters. Tony Stark was missing and presumed off-world, and now Secretary of State Ross was grilling James Rhodes—known also as War Machine—as to the whereabouts of Vision while Bruce Banner looked on.

"Still no word from Vision?" Secretary Ross asked, his holographic image flickering in through the comms system.

"Satellites lost him somewhere over Edinburgh," Rhodey answered wearily.

"On a stolen Quinjet with four of the world's most wanted criminals." Ross was speaking from the comfort of a faraway conference room, bustling with fellow cabinet members and high-ranking officials.

"You know they're only criminals because you've chosen to call them that, right, sir?" Rhodey had had enough.

"My God, Rhodes. Your talent for manipulation rivals my own," Ross spat.

"If it weren't for those Accords, Vision would've been right here."

"I remember your signature on those papers, Colonel." Ross stood, crossing to get closer to Rhodey, even if just virtually so. A move he hoped would bring home this issue once and for all.

"That's right. And I'm pretty sure I paid for that." Rhodey looked down at his paralyzed legs, another casualty of the Civil War, as people called it. Rhodey was only able to stand because his legs were now powered fully by Tony and Stark Industries.

"You have second thoughts?"

"Not anymore." Rhodey looked straight into Ross's eyes.

Both men turned to see a group of people enter the room, Captain America and Black Widow at the front; bringing up the rear, Vision, being held up by the Scarlet Witch and Falcon.

"Mr. Secretary," Cap said to the flickering ranking officer. Ross took his time to reply, walking over closer to fully take in the estranged Captain.

"You got some nerve. I'll give you that," Secretary Ross said, taking in the five new arrivals.

"You could use some of that right now," Natasha said coldly. She always stepped in, coming to Steve's aid when the proper response wasn't a respectful or polite one. Secretary Ross gave her a hard look and returned his attention to Cap.

"The world's on fire and you think all is forgiven?" Ross asked Cap pointedly.

"I'm not looking for forgiveness. And I'm way past

57

asking for permission. Earth just lost her best defender. So, we're here to fight. And if you wanna stand in our way, we'll fight you, too." Cap was adamant and unwavering. His unflinching pledge unfurled throughout the room. Secretary Ross turned away from Cap and faced Rhodey.

"Arrest them."

"All over it," Rhodey said, unmoving. Except to raise his hand and swipe Ross's flickering hologram out of the Avengers Headquarters once and for all.

"That's the court martial," Rhodey said to Cap. The moment expanded between them, and then Rhodey smiled. "It's great to see you, Cap," he said, making his way to Steve. They shook hands.

"You too, Rhodey," Steve said, trying to hide his guilt behind a genuine smile of gratitude toward his friend.

"Hey," Rhodey said to Natasha, before pulling her in for a hug. She smiled and wrapped her arms around Rhodey, happy to have at least some of the red in her ledger from the past two years accounted for.

Rhodes stepped back, looking at Cap, Black Widow, Falcon, Wanda, and Vision, all still fresh from their fight with Proxima Midnight and Corvus Glaive in Scotland. "Wow. You guys really look like crap." The time and distance he had spent apart from his former teammates began to sink in. "Must've been a rough couple . . . years."

"Yeah, well, the hotels weren't exactly five-star," Sam joked.

"I think you look great," came a familiar voice entering the lab. Bruce Banner gave a weak smile and a shrug as his teammates saw him for the first time in years. "Yeah. I'm back."

"Hi, Bruce," Natasha said softly, seeing the man she'd once hoped—maybe still hoped—would become something more than a friend.

"Nat," he replied, as discomfort filled the room. Bruce and Natasha couldn't look away from each other—there were too many unspoken words between them.

"This is awkward," Sam finally said, cutting the tension.

Bruce and the rest of the Avengers gathered in the large den-turned-war room. Bruce was as animated as ever, trying to make sure everyone understood the odds they faced. The Children of Thanos had found them once already; they could do it again. With the Time Stone somewhere in space—hopefully safe with Tony—that left the Mind Stone.

"So, we gotta assume they're coming back, right?" Sam asked.

56

"And they can clearly find us," Wanda added.

"We need all hands on deck. Where's Clint?" asked Banner, referring to Clint Barton, known also as Hawkeye.

"After the whole Accords situation, he and Scott took a deal. It was too tough on their families. They're on house arrest," Natasha said.

"Who's Scott?" Banner asked, wondering if he'd ever be fully caught up.

"Scott Lang. Ant-Man," Cap answered.

"There's an Ant-Man and a Spider-Man?" Bruce asked. "Wow. Okay, look. Thanos has the biggest army in the universe, and he's not gonna stop until he gets . . ." Bruce hesitated, taking in the wounded android. "Vision's Stone."

"Well, then, we have to protect it," Black Widow swore, stepping forward.

A quiet voice stopped all crosstalk.

"No. We have to destroy it."

All eyes turned to see Vision, staring out a window. He took a moment before looking to Cap. He gently touched the yellow Stone embedded in his head. "I've been giving a good deal of thought to this entity in my head. About its nature. But also its composition."

He walked to Wanda, knowing his words would

be met with resistance, even if it *was* the right thing to do. "I think if it were exposed to a sufficiently powerful energy source, something very similar to its own energy signature, perhaps . . ." He took her hands in his, bracing. "Perhaps its molecular integrity could fail."

Wanda looked up at him, challenging his plan immediately. "Yeah, and you with it." Her voice lowered to an intimate whisper. "We are not having this conversation."

"Eliminating the Stone is the only way to be certain that Thanos can't get it," Vision explained, as if logic had anything to do with why Wanda wouldn't even begin to entertain his plan.

Cap could only watch on hopelessly as Wanda and Vision had almost exactly the same conversation he'd had with Peggy seventy years ago when he'd put Hydra's plane down in the Arctic rather than have the Tesseract detonate and cost untold millions of human lives. He couldn't stand by and let Wanda's and Vision's lives—and futures together—spool out as his and Peggy's had. He had to find another way.

"That's too high a price," Wanda pleaded.

Vision stroked her hair. "Only you have the power to pay it." Wanda walked away from Vision as he continued speaking. "Thanos threatens half the universe." Vision turned to face the group, motioning toward himself. "One life cannot stand in the way of defeating him."

The beat of silence was broken by a commanding voice as Cap stepped forward.

"But it should." Cap shook his head. "We don't trade lives, Vision."

Vision's voice was strong. "Captain, seventy years ago you laid down your life to save how many millions of people? Tell me, why is this any different?"

Before Cap could answer, Bruce cut in. "Because you might have a choice. Your mind is made up of a complex construct of overlays: JARVIS, Ultron, Tony, me, the Stone. All of them mixed together, all of them learning from one another," Bruce explained.

"You're saying Vision isn't just the Stone?" Wanda asked, her voice cracking with tormented hope that there could be another way.

"I'm saying that if we take out the Stone, there's still a whole lot of Vision left." Banner smiled at the implications. "Perhaps the best parts."

"Can we do that?" Natasha asked.

"Not me. Not here," Bruce confessed.

"Well, you'd better find someone and somewhere fast.

Ross isn't just gonna let you guys have your old rooms back," Rhodes warned.

Luckily, Captain America was already way ahead of them.

"I know somewhere."

54

CHAPTER 9

The great Panther Statue soared high above the lush green mountains surrounding the nation of Wakanda. To the outside world, Wakanda was a country located in North East Africa known, until recently, for shepherds and textiles.

But there was much more to Wakanda than met the eye.

Wakanda was Earth's most technologically advanced city. Because it was built on top of a priceless stash of the world's most valuable and rare mineral, Vibranium, Wakanda had always chosen to conceal itself from the outside world in order to protect its precious resource. That all changed when the nation lost its monarch, T'Chaka, to a terrorist bombing at the United Nations. Wakanda now found itself under the reign of T'Chaka's son, T'Challa.

But T'Challa wouldn't serve the citizens of Wakanda only as their king. He'd also inherited the mantle of the Black Panther, and with it, had opened Wakanda's doors to the outside world at last, for better or worse.

Now, as King T'Challa strode across a field with Okoye, the general of his Dora Milaje, he was pretty certain Wakanda had entered the "for worse" part.

"The King's Guard and the Dora Milaje have been alerted."

"Send word to the Jabari as well. M'Baku likes a good fight. And what of this one?" T'Challa and Okoye approached a simple, humble hut where a one-armed man quietly worked in his fields.

"This one may be tired of war. But the White Wolf has rested long enough." One of T'Challa's King's Guards set down an elaborate case, opening it up to show the now-advancing one-armed man.

James Buchanan Barnes looked at the case with an expression of acceptance and dread. Men like Barnes didn't get to be farmers, falling asleep night after night to the quiet noises of the Wakandan countryside. No, men like Barnes heard the ticking. He knew this day would come.

When he fought at Steve Rogers's side he'd been a soldier for the Allies in World War II, but then he'd been captured by Hydra and brainwashed to be a soldier for evil. Whether he was Bucky Barnes or the Winter Soldier, he'd been fighting somebody else's war for over seventy years.

As Bucky took in the metal arm that rested inside the case, the weariness coursed through him like a disease.

"Where's the fight?" he asked, his mouth pressed into a hard line.

"On its way," T'Challa said, knowing the full weight of what he was asking.

To any other mind, especially an untrained one, panic would have set in and the person would have died instantly. The thousands of glass shards mere inches away covering their entire bodies would tear through them if they moved.

Fortunately, Doctor Stephen Strange possessed the most focused mind in the galaxy. At the moment, all that meant was that he was perfectly still, staring down said blades.

"In all the time I've served Thanos," he heard Ebony Maw brag in his melodic voice, "I have never failed him."

Maw came into Strange's line of sight. The Child of Thanos's face hardened as he inhaled sharply. "If I were to reach our rendezvous on Titan with the Time Stone still attached to your vaguely irritating person, there would be . . . judgment."

Maw leaned in to Strange as a spike shifted via his telepathy, cutting sharply into Strange's cheek with the merest touch.

"Give me the Stone."

Strange remained resilient. As punishment, more spikes began to pierce his body. He reached out with his mind to make contact with the Cloak of Levitation, which had managed to hide on Maw's ship undetected.

The Cloak floated to the deck overlooking the scene below, where Iron Man watched in horror, mind racing to formulate a plan. He jumped when the Cloak tapped him on the shoulder.

"Wow, you are a seriously loyal piece of outerwear,

aren't you?" he asked, still in shock. More surprising was the voice that came from behind in response.

"Yeah . . ." whispered Peter Parker, "uh, speaking of loyalty . . ."

"What the—" Tony's eyes flared.

"I know what you're gonna say," Peter started.

Tony cut in. "You should not be here." Tony had only continued onto the ship because he felt certain that he'd gotten Peter safely out of harm's way. With Peter here, very much IN harm's way, would he be able to fully concentrate on the task at hand?

Is this . . . oh, no . . . is this how it feels? To be on the other end of this? He owed Pepper an apology. He owed Pepper a lot of apologies.

"I was gonna go home," Peter started.

"I don't want to hear it."

"But it was such a long way down and I just thought about you on the way—"

"And now I gotta hear it."

"—and kinda stuck to the side of the ship. And this suit is ridiculously intuitive, by the way."

"Dang it, kid," Tony spat out.

"So, if anything, it's kinda your fault that I'm here." Peter rushed out the last words and braced himself. Both Tony and the Cloak of Levitation looked up in incredulity

51

at Peter's absolute presumption that this was somehow Tony's fault.

"What did you just say?" Tony's very angry face was in Peter's very embarrassed one.

"I take that back." Peter lifted his hands in surrender. "And now, I'm here in space." Tony stepped toward Peter.

"Yeah, right where I didn't want you to be." Tony leaned in and in a concerned, borderline threatening whisper, continued. "This isn't Coney Island. This isn't some field trip. This is a one-way ticket. You hear me?" Peter tried to meet his gaze, but, fully chastised, he looked down. "Don't pretend you thought this through."

Peter looked up, his tone stronger as he dug deeper for the reason he'd risked everything to stow away. "No, I did think this through."

"You could not possibly have thought this through."

"You can't be a friendly neighborhood Spider-Man if there's no neighborhood." Peter waited. "Okay, that didn't really make sense, but you know what I'm trying to say."

Tony was stuck. Peter was on this spaceship and that was that. So, he now had to save Strange and then get Peter Parker back on Earth safe and sound. But first things first.

"Come on. We got a situation." Tony sighed and pointed at Strange as the duo looked over the ledge, the Cloak hovering behind them both. "See him down there? He's in trouble. What's your plan? Go."

"Um. Okay . . . okay . . . uh . . ." Suddenly, Peter looked up and faced Tony. "Did you ever see this really old movie, *Aliens*?"

Below, Maw was circling Strange, mentally pushing individual shards into various points on the mystic's body.

"Painful, aren't they?" he mused. "They were originally designed for microsurgery." Maw turned from Strange. "And any one of them could end your friend's life in an instant." He looked up at Iron Man, who was hovering above, lasers at the ready.

"I gotta tell you, he's not really my friend. Saving his life is more of a professional courtesy."

Maw moved away from Strange and lifted massive cargo pods with a wave of his hands. "You've saved nothing. Your powers are inconsequential compared to mine!"

Iron Man shrugged. "Yeah, but the kid's seen more movies."

Tony angled himself toward the ship's side and fired a missile at the hull, its explosion tearing it open. The cargo pods flew out of the hull.

With a scream of disbelief, Ebony Maw was sucked into the coldness of space.

Chaos quickly followed. Other objects began flying out into space, including the microsurgery needles, freeing Doctor Strange. Unfortunately, Strange also began moving through the air to the opening. Just as he was about

50

to be sucked through, the Cloak of Levitation grabbed Strange's ankle with one end and a solid-looking structure with the other, holding the man in place.

Spider-Man found himself nearly sucked out when four mechanical arachnid-looking arms extended from his back like an exoskeleton. "Yes!" Peter exclaimed. "Wait. What *are* these?" He looked behind him to get a better view.

They, like the rest of the suit, acted intuitively, spreading out and gripping the hull's sides to keep Spider-Man from flying out. Peter shot a web and pulled himself and Strange to safety. With everyone safe from the hull's opening, Iron Man stepped in to weld the hole shut. Catching his breath, Peter retracted the pincers to his suit's exoskeleton and extended a hand to the Cloak of Levitation. "Hey, we haven't officially met." The Cloak considered Peter's extended hand and then floated away, toward Doctor Strange. "Cool."

"We gotta turn this ship around." Strange struggled to stand as Tony walked past, Iron Man suit disappearing as he strode.

"Yeah, now he wants to run. Great plan." Tony walked to the front of the ship, watching as the expanse of space spread out before them.

"No, I want to protect the Stone." The Cloak of Levitation encircled Strange's shoulders.

"And I want you to thank me. Now, go ahead. I'm listening."

"For what? Nearly blasting me into space?"

"Who just saved your magical butt? Me." Tony was losing his patience.

"I seriously don't know how you fit your head into that helmet," Strange marveled.

"Admit it, you should've ducked out when I told you to. I tried to bench you. You refused."

Strange gritted his teeth. "Unlike everyone else in your life, I don't work for you."

"And due to that fact, we're now in a flying doughnut billions of miles from Earth with no backup."

"I'm backup." Peter held up a single finger.

"No, you're a stowaway. The adults are talking." Tony was at his wit's end.

Strange looked bemused. "I'm sorry. I'm confused as to the relationship here. What is he, your ward?"

"No." Peter stepped forward and reached out to Doctor Strange. "I'm Peter, by the way."

"Doctor Strange."

"Oh, we're using our made-up names." Peter cleared his throat. "Um, I'm Spider-Man, then." Strange didn't bother to shake Peter's hand as he passed, his attention focused now on Tony.

49

"The ship is self-correcting its course," Tony said gravely. "Thing's on autopilot."

"Can we control it?" Strange asked, concerned. "Fly us home?" Strange reiterated. Tony's eyes flicked back to Strange. He was getting further and further lost. "Stark?" The mystic was losing his patience. "Can you get us home?"

"Yeah, I heard you." Stark waved him off. He paused to propose a new idea. "I'm thinking I'm not so sure we should."

Strange was aghast. "Under no circumstances can we bring the Time Stone to Thanos!" He paused to collect himself. "I don't think you quite understand what's at stake here."

"What?" Tony asked, stepping forward to square off against Strange. "No. It's you who doesn't understand that Thanos has been inside my head for far too long." Tony's voice was becoming more and more agitated as he spoke. "Since he sent an army to New York. And now he's back!" And then the real panic set in. "And I don't know what to do. So I'm not so sure if it's a better plan to fight him on our turf or his, but you saw what they did, what they can do. At least on his turf he's not expecting it. So I say we take the fight to him." Tony cocked his head as he looked at Strange. "Doctor, do you concur?"

There was tense silence in the room as the two men sized each other up and mulled their options. Strange raced through his mind, thinking of alternatives, wondering if Tony Stark's brash plan was possible. Tony waited, ready to stand his ground.

"All right, Stark," Strange said. "We go to him."

Tony began walking away, ready to put his plan into action. Strange wasn't done. "But you have to understand," Strange said, measured, "if it comes to saving you, or the kid, or the Time Stone, I will not hesitate to let either of you die. I can't, because the universe depends on it."

"Nice." Tony reached out and patted Strange's arm. "Good, moral compass. We're straight." Tony understood what it took to make the big choices and major sacrifices. He turned to face Peter.

"All right, kid." Peter braced himself for the worst. But instead, Tony tapped his hand on each of Peter's shoulders and mimicked knighting him. "You're an Avenger now."

Tony walked on, leaving Peter by himself. A second of disbelief passed, and then a wide, excited smile spread across his face before it dissolved into a far more resolute, serious expression. Peter nodded to himself as the honor Tony had just bestowed on him settled deep inside.

A quick blink as he pushed his shoulders back. Ready for duty. He was finally going to help make fewer bad things happen. He was going to do something meaningful with all of these powers.

He was going to make a difference.

48

CHAPTER 10

amora stood in the throne room of the *Sanctuary II*, the seat of Thanos's power and a place she was far too familiar with. She glared at the throne. Thanos approached, carrying a bowl of food.

"I thought you might be hungry," he said, handing her the bowl. Gamora looked down at the offering. She took it from Thanos, looked up at him defiantly, and threw the bowl of food against Thanos's throne.

"I always hated that chair," she spat, watching the remnants of the bowl's contents drip down.

"So I've been told," Thanos said drily. "Even so, I'd hoped you'd sit in it one day."

Gamora looked at him, fury in her eyes. "I hated this room. This ship. I hated my life!"

Thanos sat on the steps of this throne and looked at her, a sadness briefly flashing across his face. "You told me that too. Every day. For almost twenty years." There was a beat of silence between the two of them.

"I was a child when you took me," she raged.

"I saved you."

Gamora shook her head. "No. No. We were happy on my home planet."

"Going to bed hungry, scrounging for scraps. Your planet was on the brink of collapse. I'm the one who stopped that." Gamora turned from him. "Do you know what's happened since then? The children born have known nothing but full bellies and clear skies. It's a paradise," Thanos said proudly.

Whipping around, Gamora yelled, "Because you murdered half the planet!"

"A small price to pay for salvation," Thanos said.

"You're insane," Gamora growled.

"Little one, it's a simple calculation. This universe is finite, its resources finite. If life is left unchecked, life will cease to exist." He spoke calmly. "It needs correction."

"You don't know that!" Gamora shouted.

Thanos sighed and looked to the heavens. "I'm the only one who knows that. At least, I'm the only one with the will to act on it." Thanos stood and descended the stairs toward Gamora. "For a time, you had that same will as you fought by my side." Thanos loomed over her now. "Daughter."

She looked up at him. Her gaze was cold. "I am not your daughter. Everything I hate about myself, you taught me."

"And in doing so, made you the fiercest woman in the galaxy," Thanos pointed out. "That's why I trusted you to find the Soul Stone."

"I'm sorry I disappointed you," she said, her voice emotionless.

Thanos's head dropped slightly. "I am disappointed. But not because you didn't find it." He bent down in front of her, just like he'd done that first day. His voice was a low

46

growl when he next spoke. "But because you did." His eyes locked on hers. "And you lied."

Thanos led Gamora to a prison cell. Gamora couldn't hide the shock on her face when she saw who was there: Nebula. Her sister was suspended in midair; her cybernetic body was dissected into slivers and held in place, making it look as though she had been stretched apart. The room echoed with Nebula's hard-earned wheezes.

Gamora and Nebula's relationship had always been strained, to say the least. Constantly in competition, the sisters battled for their father's attention, with Gamora always being his clear favorite. And now here was her father's prized daughter invited to come gaze at the chronic screw-up once again.

Gamora looked at Nebula's twisted body and their eyes met. She became haunted by Nebula's terrified and panicked gaze. "Nebula," Gamora cried, running to her sister. Gamora turned to Thanos. "Don't do this."

"Some time ago, your sister snuck aboard this ship to kill me," Thanos started.

"Please don't do this," Gamora sobbed.

"And very nearly succeeded. So I brought her here. To talk." He flexed the Infinity Gauntlet and used the Power Stone to pull Nebula further apart, causing the would-be assassin to scream.

"Stop. Stop it." Gamora went to Thanos and placed a hand on his Gauntleted hand. Her touch was familiar and easy. She looked up at him. "I swear to you on my life. I never found the Soul Stone."

Thanos looked to a guard. The guard pressed a few buttons.

"Accessing memory files," a computer voice intoned. A flickering grainy hologram emanated from Nebula and played out like a nightmare in front of Gamora.

"You know what he's about to do. He's finally ready and he's going for the Stones. All of them." Nebula's voice from long ago filtered through the room.

"He can never get them all." The holographic Gamora stood brazenly, arms crossed.

"He will!" Nebula had screamed.

"He can't, Nebula. Because I found the map to the Soul Stone, and I burned it to ash. I burned it." Thanos stood over the very real Gamora as the hologram disappeared. She was collapsing in on herself as he began to speak.

"You're strong. Me. You're generous. Me." He stood behind her now. "But I never taught you to lie. That's why you're so bad at it." Still standing behind her, he extended his Gauntleted hand past Gamora. His fingers lazily waved around as he spoke each word.

"Where is the Soul Stone?" he asked again. Gamora shook her head. She wouldn't. She couldn't.

45

Thanos curled his fingers into a tight fist. Nebula watched helplessly as the Stones shone bright. The ensuing pain was like nothing she'd ever felt. Nebula writhed and shrieked in pain as each second lasted a year and all she could do was wish for death.

Gamora watched as her sister thrashed against their father's punishment, weighing the cost of one life against billions. But it was her sister and she couldn't bear listening to Nebula's agonized howls for one more moment. Gamora remained quiet, keeping the Soul Stone's whereabouts a mystery from her father. Sensing Gamora's hesitation, Thanos tightened his fist and the sickening sound of Nebula's body being stretched beyond its limits filled the room.

"Vormir!" Gamora yelled. Thanos relaxed his hand and Nebula's screams stopped, only to yield to her ragged heaving as she tried to catch her breath. Gamora walked over to Nebula and placed her hand on the side of her sister's tear-stained face. Nebula just shook her head, guilt-ridden that it was her life that Thanos had used to torture the Soul Stone's location out of Gamora. "The Stone is on Vormir," Gamora said more quietly.

Thanos smiled, opening a teleportation portal.

"Show me."

"I am Groot," Groot said, squirming in his chair.

"Tinkle in the cup. We're not looking. What's there to see? What's a twig? Everybody's seen a twig before."

"I am Groot." Groot's voice was increasingly panicked.

"Tree, pour what's in the cup out into space and go in the cup again," Thor said, turning to the wriggling sapling.

"You speak Groot?" Rocket asked, turning around in his captain's chair.

"Yes, they taught it on Asgard. It was an elective."

"I am Groot," Groot said, now bored now that he was no longer panicked about needing to pee.

"You'll know when we're close. Nidavellir's force harnesses the blazing power of a neutron star." Thor stepped away from the window and sat down wearily on a step, his head hung low. "It's the birthplace of my hammer. It's truly awesome." Rocket spun back around, hearing the flatness in Thor's voice.

"Okay, time to be a captain." Rocket put on the autopilot, undid his seat belt, and walked over to Thor. He busied himself with some coordinates on a readout as he spoke. "So, dead brother, huh? Yeah, that could be annoying."

"Well, he's been dead before. But, no, this time I think it really might be true," Thor said, as if coming to terms with it just in that very moment.

"And you said your sister and your dad?"

44

"Both dead," Thor said, shaking his head.

"But still got a mom, though?"

"Killed by a dark elf." Thor couldn't look at Rocket.

"A best friend?"

"Stabbed through the heart." Thor's voice was detached as he rattled off all the people he'd lost. He was growing more and more melancholy.

Rocket stepped closer. "You sure you're up for this particular murder mission?"

"Absolutely." Thor brushed away Rocket's concern with a forced laugh. "Rage and vengeance, anger, loss, regret. They're all tremendous motivators. They really clear the mind. So, I'm good to go."

"Yeah, but this Thanos we're talkin' about . . . he's the toughest there is."

"Well, he's never fought me."

"Yeah, he has." Rocket pointed out the obvious.

Thor considered Rocket's response. "He's never fought me twice. And I'm getting a new hammer, don't forget."

"It better be some hammer." Rocket's words washed over Thor and the forced laugh crumbled into a sorrow that was rooted deep in Thor's bones. He struggled to find his footing. He couldn't let this get to him.

"You know, I'm fifteen hundred years old. I've killed twice as many enemies as that. And every one of them would've rather killed me, but none succeeded. I'm only alive because fate wants me alive. Thanos is just the latest in a long line of bastards and he'll be the latest to feel my vengeance. Fate wills it so."

"And what if you're wrong?" Rocket's question hit Thor in the chest. But it was the answer that took his breath away.

"If I'm wrong, then what more could I lose?" Thor's words felt vast as he swiped away a mutinous tear. He got up and walked away from Rocket before he was forced to face any more dismal truths about what used to be his full and wonderful life.

"I could lose a lot," Rocket muttered to himself. "Me, personally, I could lose a lot." Rocket pulled something from his vest. "Okay." Rocket walked over to Thor. "Well, if fate does want you to kill that crapsack, you're gonna need more than one stupid eyeball." Rocket handed him the gift.

"What's this?" Thor took it.

"What's it look like? Some jerk lost a bet with me on Contraxia." Rocket climbed back up into the captain's chair, buckled in, and turned off autopilot.

"He gave you his eye?"

"No, he gave me a hundred credits. I snuck into his room later that night and stole the eye."

"Thank you, sweet rabbit." Thor peeled off his eye patch just as Groot leaned over, intrigued by what was

43

quickly turning into something way more interesting than that video game. Thor spread his eye socket wide and popped in the new eye.

"I would've washed that. The only way I could sneak it off Contraxia was up my—" An alarm blared through the ship. "Hey, we're here!"

Thor focused his new eye as it calibrated itself to its new owner, whacking the side of his head. "I don't think this thing works. Everything seems dark." Thor stood and stared out the ship's front window.

"It ain't the eye." Eerie darkness surrounded them.

"Something's wrong. The star's gone out. And the rings are frozen."

Whatever Rocket had hoped to see when he reached Nidavellir vanished like the light of the neutron star the great forge once held. Rocket carefully navigated their ship to the star's surface.

The trio landed and exited the ship, and as Thor walked among the forge's ruins, he was haunted by what could have caused this.

"I hope these dwarves are better at forging than they are at cleaning. Maybe they realized that they live in a junk pile in the middle of space."

"This forge hasn't gone dark in centuries," said the Asgardian.

Rocket gulped audibly. He was looking down at something — the possible answer to the mystery of why Nidavellir was in the state of ruin.

"You said Thanos had a Gauntlet, right?" Rocket called out to Thor.

"Yes, why?"

Thor walked over to see what Rocket had found. "It look anything like that?"

A mold, the only one left intact as far as they could see, was lying next to the forging basin. It was in the shape of a large glove with six insets. There was no doubt — they were at the birthplace of the Infinity Gauntlet.

"I am Groot!" came a sharp warning from the teen-aged treelike creature.

"Get back to the pod," Thor commanded, fearing the worst. But it was too late. A giant with long, shaggy hair and a dark bushy beard appeared out of nowhere. He kicked Thor across the forge, turned, and did the same to Groot and Rocket. The giant advanced on Thor, and through that mussed mane of hair, Thor saw murder in his eyes.

"Eitri, wait!" The large creature paused at the sound of his name. "Stop!" Thor's voice repeated the word, calmingly. "Stop."

Eitri the Dwarf, keeper of the forge at Nidavellir, maker of Mjolnir, halted in his tracks. His clothes were

42

tattered. His hair was tangled. He looked as though he had not slept in months, and smelled like his last bath had been even longer ago.

"Thor?" Eitri's voice was tinged with recognition, as though he was coming out of a fog.

Thor approached his longtime friend. "What happened here?"

"You were supposed to protect us. Asgard was supposed to protect us," Eitri howled in grief.

"Asgard is destroyed." Thor stood and pointed back at the Gauntlet mold. "Eitri, the glove. What did you do?"

The dwarf looked around; shame and regret filled his face. Eitri stumbled over to the forge and slid to the floor in defeat. "Three hundred dwarves lived on this ring. I thought if I did what he asked, they'd be safe. I made what he wanted, a device capable of harnessing the power of the Stones." Despair now tinged every word. "Then he k . . . then he killed everyone anyway. All except me."

It was then that Thor noticed Eitri's hands were gnarled and encased in unbreakable steel.

" 'Your life is yours,' he said, 'but your hands are mine alone.' "

Thor's voice was strong, commanding, and his attitude assuring. "Eitri, this isn't about your hands. Every weapon you've ever designed, every ax, hammer, sword . . . it's all inside your head. Now, I know it feels like all hope is lost. Trust me, I know. But together, you and I . . ." The Odinson made Eitri's eyes meet his and spoke a vow that stirred in Eitri's heart.

"We can kill Thanos."

Half a galaxy away, the *Sanctuary II* hovered in deep space. It housed those who believed in Thanos's cause, the many races who served in his armies, and hundreds of guards dedicated to protecting him, even if he was off-board, as he was now.

One such guard was put in charge of piecing back together the mangled body that used to be Thanos's second-favorite daughter, Nebula. He encircled her as she hung in her suspended prison state, pushing and twisting parts of her back to where they were prior to her father ripping her apart tendon by tendon. He heard a whir and saw her cybernetic eye had extended. They were under the strictest of orders to make sure nothing happened to Nebula until Thanos returned from Vormir. The guard investigated the cybernetic eye.

Her trap sprung, Nebula quickly overcame the guard. As his body hit the floor she thought to herself, *Be thankful you won't have to face Thanos when he finds me gone.* Focusing on the task at hand, Nebula raced to the comms station inside her cell. She punched in familiar coordinates.

Before those on the other end could acknowledge

they'd received her call, Nebula hushed them. Leaning in, Nebula whispered to her sometime teammate.

"Mantis, listen very carefully. I need you to meet me on Titan."

"Hey, what's going on?" Peter Parker asked, as the flying doughnut they were on began to feel more like it was careening for Titan than landing on Titan.

"I think we're here," Strange said, watching as the planet closed in at an alarmingly fast rate.

"I don't think this rig has a self-park function," Tony said. He hurried over to Peter and pushed him toward one of the steering mechanisms. "Get your hand inside the steering gimbal. Close those around it. You understand?" Tony set himself up in the other one.

"Yep, got it." Peter did as he was told.

"This was meant for one big guy, so we gotta move at the same time." Always the mentor, even while asking his student to help land a giant doughnut on a faraway planet.

"Okay, okay. Ready." Peter watched in horror as their ship pitched and sped directly toward the giant starlike structures that peppered Titan's landscape.

"We might wanna turn. Turn! Turn! Turn!" Tony activated his suit for more power, as did Peter. But nothing helped. The ship was crashing. Strange stepped forward and conjured a golden force field around all three of them as the ship snapped in two and fell to the planet's surface.

Titan was a place haunted by its long-ago grandeur, now ruins built upon ruins. Star-shaped structures littered the area; ash and dust filled the air as though the planet was aflame. The pale red sky only added to the apocalyptic feeling. There were pockets where gravity barely existed, causing dust and debris to hang in the air, like a grave surrounding them.

"You all right?" Strange ran over to Tony, still struggling in the wreckage of what was left of Ebony Maw's ship. Strange extended a hand. Tony gladly took it and let the mystic help him up to a standing position, a far cry from where the two had been previously.

"That was close," said Tony. Strange nodded, looking around at what was left of the ship. "I owe you one."

Peter lowered himself from what was left of the ceiling of the ship and began rambling. "Let me just say, if aliens wind up implanting eggs in my chest or something and I eat one of you, I'm sorry—"

Tony cut Peter off, pointing a disciplinary finger up at the boy. "I do not want another single pop culture reference out of you for the rest of the trip. You understand?" Tony scolded.

"I'm trying to say that something is coming," Peter blurted.

40

Before they could react, a metal ball rolled in between all three of them and exploded, sending Strange and Tony flying.

From behind an outcropping, the Guardians of the Galaxy sprang to action.

"Thanos!" Drax yelled as he threw his twin blades at Strange. A quick flick of Strange's wrist and a magical whip disarmed the charging green-skinned Drax. Before Drax could recover, the Cloak of Levitation easily pinned the muscular Drax to the ground.

Iron Man took to the sky, dodging blasts from the masked Star-Lord. The two exchanged fire, each deftly dodging and blocking the other's blows in midair. It looked like Iron Man had the upper hand, until Star-Lord planted a powerful magnet on Tony's RT, which left him stuck and squirming against a twisted piece of metal.

"Please don't put your eggs in me," Peter howled as he backed away from Mantis, shooting webs as he swerved and looped to evade her.

"Stay down, clown," Star-Lord yelled, kicking him away from entrapping Mantis any further. Spider-Man rolled away, activating his exoskeleton of four spider legs, hopping and swinging around the ship's wreckage, dodging Star-Lord's blasts.

Drax wrestled with the Cloak, trying to both free

himself and contain the sentient cloth. "Die, blanket of death!" he bellowed.

Tony finally freed himself, flew over to the embattled Drax, and loomed over him, weapons fully activated. Seeing this, Star-Lord grabbed Spider-Man and pulled him in, holding his blaster to the side of the boy's head.

"Everybody stay where you are. Chill the eff out," he said. Quill reached up and deactivated his mask. He turned to Iron Man. "I'm gonna ask you this one time: Where's Gamora?"

"Yeah," Tony challenged. "I'll do you one better: Who's Gamora?" He raised his faceplate.

Still pinned to the ground by the Cloak of Levitation, Drax waxed philosophical. "I'll do you one better: *Why* is Gamora?"

"Tell me where the girl is or I swear to you I'm gonna french fry this little freak." Quill pushed his blaster harder against Spider-Man's skull.

"Let's do it. You shoot my guy and I'll blast him. Let's go!" Tony yelled, calling Quill's bluff. But however much bravado Tony seemed to have, the dread of exactly this moment was laced in his words. He was terrified. Pushing through his fear, Tony held a particularly menacing-looking weapon inches from Drax's face.

"Do it, Quill! I can take it." Drax lifted his hands in surrender and braced himself.

"No, he can't take it," Mantis yelled.

"She's right. You can't," Strange agreed, flicking his gaze over to Drax.

"Oh yeah? You don't want to tell me where she is? That's fine. I'll kill all three of you and I'll beat it out of Thanos myself. Starting with you." Quill tightened his grip on Spider-Man.

"Wait, what, Thanos? All right, let me ask you this one time. What master do you serve?" Strange asked, his voice breathless as it cut through the chaos.

"What master do I serve? What am I supposed to say, Jesus?" Quill's frustrated sigh could be heard back in New York. Tony stared at him, a realization beginning to crystallize.

"You're from Earth," Tony stated, his face creased with hidden terror at this idiot still pressing his blaster to Spider-Man's head.

"I'm not from Earth, I'm from Missouri."

"Yeah, that's on Earth, moron. What are you hassling us for?" Tony barked, completely frustrated.

"You're not with Thanos?" Spider-Man asked, his voice muffled and tiny.

"With Thanos? No, I'm here to kill Thanos. He took my girl. Wait, who are you?" Quill finally lowered his blaster. The loss of Gamora had made him feel as though he was going crazy, and he was having trouble keeping anything straight in his mind except that he needed to find the woman he loved.

"We're the Avengers, man," Peter said, finally revealing his face.

"You're the ones Thor told us about," Mantis said, her voice loud and panicked.

Those words stopped Iron Man in his tracks. "You know Thor?"

"Yeah. Tall guy, not that good-looking, needed saving," Quill said, trying to keep his voice level.

Knowing that Thor had survived Thanos's attack, possibly one of the only creatures to have done so, piqued Doctor Strange's interest. He must speak with Thor; he felt the Asgardian had a very important role in the tapestry that was unfolding.

"Where is he now?"

The darkened forge of Nidavellir held many secrets in its depths. Eitri held one such secret close. It was an ancient mold, a cast. On one end was the shape of an ax, on the other the shape of a hammer.

Rocket looked unimpressed. "This is the plan? We're gonna hit him with a rock?"

Giving Rocket a withering glare, Eitri explained. "It's a mold. A king's weapon. Meant to be the greatest in Asgard. In theory, it could even summon the Bifrost."

At the mention of this weapon, and the possibility of wielding the Bifrost, Thor turned quickly. If they could use this weapon to cross the Nine Realms, he could race Thanos to Earth and stop him.

"Did it have a name?" Thor asked.

"Stormbreaker."

Rocket scoffed. "That's a bit much."

Thor had studied all of Asgardian lore when it came to weapons. This was something thought only to be legend. Until now. "So how do we make it?"

At this, Eitri's face fell. "You'll have to restart the forge. Awaken the heart of a dying star."

Thor accepted the challenge, an idea forming. Turning to Rocket, he nodded to the ship's captain. "Rabbit, fire up the pod."

On Titan, the Guardians and the Avengers were attempting to come to a meeting of the minds.

"The hell happened to this planet? It's eight degrees off its axis. Gravitational pull is all over the place," Quill said as he stepped gingerly among the crumbling ruins of the decimated surface.

"Yeah, we've got one advantage: he's coming to us," said Tony. In the background Mantis jumped and spun high into the air, taking advantage of the planet's bizarre gravity. Tony continued, "We'll use it. All right, I have a plan." He walked over to Quill. "Or the beginnings of one. It's pretty simple. We draw him in, pin him down, get what we need. Definitely don't wanna dance with this guy. We just want the Gauntlet." It was simple, but it was a start.

Then he heard Drax yawn.

Tony was infuriated. "Are you yawning? In the middle of this, while I'm breaking it down? Huh? Did you hear what I said?"

"I stopped listening after you said 'We need a plan.'"

"Okay, Mr. Clean is on his own page," Tony said, ready to hurry this whole thing along.

"See, 'not winging it' isn't really what we do," Quill explained.

"What exactly is it that you do?" Spider-Man asked, pointing at Mantis and Drax.

"Kick names, take butt," Mantis said, her voice a "menacing" roar.

"Yeah, that's right," Drax agreed, standing taller.

Tony stared at the two for a long time.

A long time.

They were about to take on the greatest enemy they'd ever faced. This was an enemy that had haunted Tony for six years. An enemy that threatened to wipe out half of the universe, untold trillions of beings with the snap of his fingers. And he was on an apocalyptic, dead planet millions of miles from home with none of his usual partners. He was

37

in the fight of his life and he was utterly alone. No, he was worse than alone. He had a wide-eyed kid he had to protect, an arrogant magician, and now these three idiots who appeared to be just cocky enough to get them all killed.

"All right, just get over here, please. Mr. Lord, can you get your folks to circle up?"

"'Mr. Lord.' Star-Lord is fine." Quill gave Mantis and Drax a nod and they stepped forward.

Tony addressed the group. "We gotta coalesce. 'Cause if all we come at him with is a plucky attitude—"

"Dude, don't call us plucky. We don't know what it means." Quill said. Tony glared at Quill. How could this be getting worse? "All right, we're optimistic, yes. I like your plan. Except, it sucks—so let *me* do the plan and that way it might be really good."

"Tell him about the dance-off to save the universe," Drax said proudly.

"What dance-off?" Tony asked.

"It's nothing," Quill lied.

"Like in *Footloose*, the movie?" Peter Parker asked.

"Exactly like *Footloose*. Is it still the greatest movie in history?" Quill asked, awestruck.

"It never was." Parker's flippant, careless words struck Quill in the heart.

"Don't encourage this, all right?" Tony said to the newest Avenger.

"Okay," Peter whispered.

"We're getting help from Flash Gordon here," Tony said under his breath.

"Flash Gordon?" said Quill. "By the way, that's a compliment. Don't forget I'm half human. So that fifty percent of me that's stupid, that's one hundred percent of you."

"Your math is blowing my mind," Tony fired back, before Mantis interrupted.

"Excuse me, but does your friend often do that?" she asked, pointing to Doctor Strange.

Strange was seated cross-legged, floating in midair. His hands were formed in a strange gesture and the Time Stone shone bright green. Most disturbing, however, was how quickly his head was moving back and forth. It was so rapid his face was a blur.

"Strange? We all right?" Tony called up to him.

Just as they walked up to him, the frantic motion stopped as his body crashed to the ground. Tony bent down to help him up, just as Strange had done back in Ebony Maw's now-destroyed ship.

Slowly coming out of his trance, Strange placed his hand on Tony's shoulder, raising himself to a seated position. He was breathing heavily, as though he had just awoken from a nightmare.

"You're back," Tony assured him. "You're all right."

"Hi," Strange groaned to Tony, collecting himself.

36

"Hey, um, what was that?" Spider-Man asked, his curiosity getting the better of him.

Trying to regain his composure, Doctor Strange addressed the group. "I went forward in time to view alternate futures." He took a slight gasp, the effort and his visions having clearly taken much out of him. "To see all the possible outcomes of the coming conflict."

Quill broke the silence as he nervously asked, "How many did you see?"

"Fourteen million, six hundred and five," Strange answered.

Tony, afraid to ask, voiced the only thing on anyone's mind. "How many did we win?"

Strange took a long time to answer. His eyes locked on Tony. His voice was hoarse when he spoke the single word that put an end to whatever power struggle had been happening between the two of them, the Guardians, or anyone else.

"One."

On the other side of the universe floated a lonely planet and its single moon, orbiting a dark sun: Vormir. Long devoid of life, any claims to glory the planet once had were now gone. There was only one reason anyone came to Vormir. The dark sky with a crimson tint caused by a slow solar eclipse happening backlit the mountain peak in the distance. Even though it was miles away on foot, Thanos and Gamora could still see the two towers built high on the top of the mountain.

"The Stone had better be up there. For your sister's sake," Thanos swore.

After a long trek up the mountain, the father and daughter came to the mouth of what appeared to be a cave. The darkness shifted in the wind and revealed it was actually a tunnel.

"Welcome, Thanos, son of A'Lars. Gamora, daughter of Thanos," came a voice from the darkness.

"You know us?" Thanos called out to the voice.

"It is my curse to know all who journey here." An ethereal floating figure appeared, roughly the size of a human man, robed, its face hidden by the hood.

"Where is the Soul Stone?" Thanos asked, not wanting to play games when he was so close to achieving what had evaded so many others. If the tales were true.

"You should know," the voice said, like a dark storm, "it exacts a terrible price."

Thanos stepped forward. "I am prepared."

"We all think that at first." With that, the figure pulled back its hood, revealing the hollowed scarlet face of Red Skull beneath. "We are all wrong."

With that, Red Skull led them through the tunnel and between the two towers to a ritualistic temple. It lay in ruins, boulders having crushed parts of it. Storms and

35

lightning had scorched the ground and walls. "How is it you know this place so well?" Thanos asked.

"A lifetime ago, I, too, sought the Stones. I even held one in my hand. But it cast me out, banished me here. Guiding others to a treasure I cannot possess." Red Skull led Thanos and Gamora to a sharp cliff, the bottom of which was too far down to see. As Thanos and Gamora carefully stepped closer, Red Skull continued, "What you seek lies in front of you. As does what you fear."

"What is this?" Gamora asked, her voice catching in her throat as she looked over the cliff's edge.

"The price. Soul holds a special place among the Infinity Stones. You might say it has a certain wisdom," Red Skull answered.

"Tell me what it needs." Thanos had waited long enough.

"To ensure that whoever possesses it understands its power, the Stone demands a sacrifice."

"Of what?" Thanos asked.

"In order to take the Stone, you must lose that which you love."

Thanos turned away from the cliff's edge to look back at Red Skull. He'd already sacrificed so much. What could the Stone possibly take that he hadn't already lost?

"A soul for a soul."

At these words, Thanos's eyes began to well with tears.

Gamora began laughing. It felt good, if just for this moment, to know she could still laugh. Thanos had robbed her of such frivolous emotions her whole life, but now to smile and feel this swell of fairness and relief made Gamora believe that maybe . . . maybe she had a shot. Maybe she could have a future filled with love after all. She thought of Quill and her heart soared. She'd rescue Nebula and free her. And maybe Nebula would even want to join their little dysfunctional family back on the Guardians' ship. Drax and Mantis. Rocket and Groot. Gamora was so different from her father. She'd known love. She'd found a family. And, as messy as it was certainly going to be, for the first time in her life, Gamora felt hope.

Gamora began to speak. "All my life I dreamed of a day, a moment, when you got what you deserved. And I was always so disappointed." She stepped toward Thanos, looking him directly in the eye. "But now . . . You kill and torture and you call it mercy." She gave a bitter laugh. "The universe has judged you. You asked it for a prize, and it told you no. You failed. And do you wanna know why? Because you love nothing. No one."

Thanos turned to face Gamora, tears streaming down his face. "No."

Gamora scoffed. "Really? Tears?"

Red Skull's haunting voice echoed across the still land. "They're not for him."

34

Looking at Red Skull, a realization began to set in for Gamora. Her mind went blank. Her hope vanished. Her joy evaporated. Her future—no. Disbelief. Rage. How could this be happening? She looked up at Thanos in a fury.

Thanos advanced on Gamora.

"No," she said, shakily. "This isn't love."

"I ignored my destiny once. I cannot do that again. Even for you." Thanos's words choked in his throat.

Gamora hung her head. This was all her fault. She had let herself be taken in by this monster, let him form a bond with her that was enough for him to call it love. This was all her fault. She looked up at him. Boldly. There was no hope for her now.

All she could do was make this right.

Quickly, Gamora reached into Thanos's vest, grabbed his knife and, with all her might, drove it into her chest. But before the knife could penetrate her skin, it disappeared, bubbles floating up from her hands instead. She watched them fly away, and her last vestige of hope with them.

"I'm sorry, little one," Thanos said, tears still streaming down his face. He grabbed Gamora by the arm and dragged her toward the edge of the cliff. She fought him bravely, punching and scratching and kicking to free herself. With every blow she landed, Thanos wept. Finally, unable to take the pain of losing the one thing he loved for a moment longer, he flung his daughter over the side of the cliff. As she fell, she reached up for him, calling out to him. He watched in stunned silence as her body hit the slate gray slab hundreds of feet below, landing like a broken rag doll.

A bright white light flashed, illuminating the sky, blinding Thanos and transporting him to another space and time. Tranquil and motionless, the world felt like a dream. The power of the Soul Stone was released. Thanos lifted himself from a shallow pool of water, a glowing, golden-orange Stone now sitting in his hand.

PART FOUR

28

CHAPTER 11

"Drop to 2,600, heading zero-three-zero," Cap said to Sam.

"I hope you're right about this," Sam said, as he set the coordinates of the Quinjet toward what looked to be the side of a mountain. "Or we're gonna land a lot faster than you want to."

The Quinjet sped up, aiming itself directly into the mountainside. But as Sam braced himself for impact, the Quinjet passed though the rock surface and beyond a beehive-like transparent dome to the Kingdom of Wakanda that was hidden behind it.

The great nation of Wakanda, a technological marvel the world had never heard of until recently, had spent the past two days preparing for war. Not just any war, though. They had recently faced a war that had threatened their own nation from within, and survived it; but this threat could destroy more than just their nation—this was an intergalactic threat with the fate of trillions hanging in the balance. And Wakanda was going to be Ground Zero of the battle that decided the fate of half the beings in the universe.

"When you said we were going to open Wakanda to the rest of the world, this is not what I imagined," Okoye muttered under her breath as she and T'Challa advanced briskly to meet their arriving guests. T'Challa's Dora Milaje followed closely behind the duo as they strode across the tarmac.

"And what did you imagine?" T'Challa asked, his playful smile spreading.

"The Olympics. Maybe even a Starbucks."

The Quinjet touched down on the royal landing pad and the occupants streamed out. Steve Rogers led the group, locking eyes with his old friend.

"Should we bow?" Banner asked Rhodey under his breath.

"Yeah, he's a king," Rhodey said.

Steve and T'Challa greeted each other warmly. "It seems I'm always thanking you for something," Steve said, extending his hand. T'Challa took it and the two shook in a warm grasp; an unspoken bond of mutual respect earned on the field of battle existed between them. Now, once again, they stood on such a field. Banner cleared his throat as he began to kneel.

"We don't do that here," T'Challa remonstrated him gently. Banner looked over accusingly at Rhodey, who couldn't help but smile.

"So, how big of an assault should we expect?" T'Challa asked Cap.

Bruce stepped forward. "Sir, I think you should expect quite a big assault."

24

"How we looking?" Natasha asked, inquiring about T'Challa's defenses. T'Challa nodded, calculating in his mind. "You will have my King's Guard, the Border Tribe, the Dora Milaje, and . . ." His voice trailed off as he noticed Steve Rogers's gaze shift to something behind him.

Some*one*.

"And a semi-stable hundred-year-old man," said Bucky Barnes. The Winter Soldier's prosthetic arm was now equipped with Vibranium technology, courtesy of T'Challa. Steve thought that Bucky looked well. More important, he looked calm. His eyes had a sense of clarity to them that Steve hadn't seen in years. He looked like the old Bucky Barnes that Steve first knew back in Brooklyn all those years ago. He'd gotten his best friend back.

Cap's eyes lit up as he approached Bucky, pulling his friend into a tight hug, a genuine smile stretched across his face. The first in a long time. "How you been, Buck?"

Bucky grinned back. "Not bad . . . for the end of the world."

Deep in the heart of Mount Bashenga was the central brain system of Wakandan technology—both literally and figuratively. The Wakandan Design Group was responsible for what made Wakanda the most advanced society on the planet. The head of the group, a young girl who happened to be the princess of Wakanda and T'Challa's sister—Shuri—was the brains behind practically every design.

"The structure is polymorphic," Shuri said to the assembled group of Avengers who were huddled in her lab. While she examined the Mind Stone's connection on Vision's head, Vision was lying on a surgical table in the center of it all. Shuri used a Kimoyo bead to scan Vision and the Mind Stone, projecting a holographic image of the intricate pattern that the Stone had traced to embed itself in Vision's brain.

"Right, we had to attach each neuron nonsequentially," Bruce explained.

Banner was trying to hide his awe at the young woman's genius . . . and his envy of the lab's technology. The scientist in him was in heaven, and he was finally able to contribute to the fight in an active way.

"Why didn't you just reprogram the synapses to work collectively?" Shuri asked, as if it was the simplest of processes. Vision looked from Shuri to Banner.

"Because we didn't think of it." Banner blushed.

"I'm sure you did your best," Shuri said charitably.

Wanda took Vision's hand and looked nervously at Shuri. "Can you do it?"

The young genius looked around to all assembled. "Yes, but there are more than two trillion neurons here. One misalignment could cause a cascade of circuit failures."

23

Shuri looked to T'Challa. "It will take time, brother." T'Challa nodded, understanding the magnitude of what Shuri was saying.

"How long?" Steve asked, a promise in his voice that he would personally ensure that Shuri had the time she needed.

"As long as you can give me," she replied.

At that moment, Okoye's bracelet lit up. Tapping one of the Kimoyo beads, a holograph appeared. She steeled her eyes as she looked around the room.

"Something's entered the atmosphere."

The war had begun.

"Hey, Cap. We've got a situation here," Sam said, as he and Bucky watched a plume of smoke trace from high above while a monolith of a ship descended just overhead. The ship hit the shields above the Golden City—the capital of Wakanda—and exploded.

"God, I love this place," Bucky observed in awe, looking at the glitching blue-hued Wakandan defense system.

"Don't start celebrating yet, guys. We've got more incoming outside the dome," Rhodey radioed.

A second volley of ships landed outside the dome, their sharp ends piercing the ground like spikes, causing the land around the dome to look as though it were under siege by an armada of multistory square columns.

The tremors that followed were felt all over Wakanda

and the trees began to quake. The unmistakable sound of an army on the march grew closer and closer.

"It's too late," Vision said to those in the lab. He began to climb off the table, his earlier plan seeming to be the most logical in his mind. "We need to destroy the Stone now."

"Vision, get your butt back on the table," Black Widow barked.

"We will hold them off," the Black Panther assured him.

Everyone save Shuri, Vision, and the Scarlet Witch turned to leave. "Wanda, as soon as that Stone's out of his head, you blow it to hell," Cap said. He squeezed her shoulder for moral support.

"I will," she promised.

The Black Panther turned to Okoye. "Evacuate the city. Engage all defenses," he ordered. Then, pointing to Steve Rogers, he added, "And get this man a shield."

Back on Nidavellir, Rocket flew the pod away from the forge and toward the dead star. As they hovered over the frozen rings, Thor stood outside of the pod, a cable tied around his waist.

"I don't think you get the scientifics here. These rings are gigantic. You wanna get them moving, you're going to need something a lot bigger to yank 'em loose," Rocket warned, hovering just above the frozen rings. Thor leaped down from the pod and onto the rings.

22

"Leave it to me," Thor said, gripping the cable.

"Leave it to you? Buddy, you're in space. All you got is a rope and a—" Rocket was cut off by a powerful whipping noise as Thor began to swing the pod around with the might of a Thunder God.

"Fire the engine!" Thor yelled, and Rocket did as he was told, firing the pod's engines as high as they could go, pulling Thor along behind it. Thor skidded along the frozen ring, finally digging his heels into the metal and hanging on to the cable for dear life.

"More power, rabbit!" Thor dug in his heels and let the tiny pod's power force the frozen rings to move. Rocket pushed the pod harder than he ever had, his face contorted in pure effort and concentration while the ship whined beneath him in protest. Thor let out a primal scream as the ice that had formed around the frozen ring's mechanisms began to crack and yield. A deep rumble issued from beneath Thor as the frozen rings yawned to life. The rings aligned and the brilliant light of the once-dead star shone like a beacon of hope throughout the universe.

"Well done, boy," Eitri said, amazed at the once-again bright, shining star.

Thor jumped onto the pod and pressed himself against the windshield. "That's Nidavellir!" Thor yelled to Rocket through the windshield of the little pod that could. Rocket gazed upon the brilliant star in speechless awe.

A beam of light shot from the star, through the now aligned rings and straight into the heart of the forge. Eitri gazed around, as the forge came to life once again. For a few seconds, all was well.

Until something went wrong, and the beam of light disappeared. Once again, the forge went cold.

"Dang it," Eitri spat out.

"Dang it? What's dang it?" Rocket asked.

"The mechanism is crippled," Eitri explained.

"What?" Thor asked.

"With the iris closed, I can't heat the metal," Eitri explained.

"How long will it take to heat it?" Thor asked, exhaustion evident in his tone.

"A few minutes? Maybe more. Why?" Eitri answered.

"I'm going to hold it open." Thor stood, readying himself for another round.

"That's suicide," Eitri warned.

"So is facing Thanos without that ax," Thor bit back, resolved.

And with that, Thor leaped into the center of the iris.

"How we looking, Bruce?" Black Widow asked.

"Yeah, I think I'm getting the hang of it." Wearing his Hulkbuster armor, Bruce bounded across the green fields, leaping over the tops of the Wakandan warriors in their

21

transports on the way to the front line. "Wahooo!" Bruce began to run along with the army transports. "Wow, this is amazing, man. It's like being the Hulk without actually being—" Bruce's words were cut off as he tripped heavily over an errant rock. Okoye rode past, side-eyeing Bruce's now grass-stained, squirming robotic body with disdain.

"I'm okay." Bruce pulled chunks of dirt and grass from the suit's helmet. "I'm okay."

"I've got two heat signatures breaking through the tree line," War Machine said, crackling through the radio as he and Falcon soared high over the Wakandan armies.

Proxima Midnight and Cull Obsidian ambled up to the shield just as the Wakandan tribes got into formation.

"Ah! Oou! Oou!"

"Male faa!"

"Ah! Oou! Oou!"

"Male faa!"

The Jabari chant could be heard by all as the warriors and their leader, M'Baku, exchanged proclamations, letting T'Challa know that M'Baku had answered the call to join them in the fight to save the world.

"Thank you for standing with us," T'Challa said, taking M'Baku's arm in his. M'Baku looked down at T'Challa, now suited up as the Black Panther, and nodded respectfully.

"Mfowethu," M'Baku said in Xhosa. His words simply translated to, *My brother.*

Marching to the edge of the barrier with Black Widow and Bruce Banner in the Hulkbuster armor, Captain America and the Black Panther faced Proxima Midnight and Cull Obsidian. Proxima ran her weapon along the shield, testing its limits. As the barrier hummed between them, the two sides stood mere feet apart.

"Where's your other friend?" Natasha taunted.

"You will pay for his life with yours." Proxima turned her attention to Cap and the Black Panther. "Thanos will have that Stone."

"That's not gonna happen," Steve swore.

T'Challa's commanding voice carried across so all could hear. "You are in Wakanda now. Thanos will have nothing but dust and blood."

Proxima Midnight's smile was chilling. "We have blood to spare." She raised her weapon with a howl.

"They surrender?" Bucky asked Cap as he returned to the front line.

"Not exactly," Steve said with a worried shrug.

"Yibambe!" T'Challa called to his troops. His chant simply meant, *Stop!*

"Yibambe!" The answer came from the thousands who fought.

20

"Yibambe!" T'Challa called out again.

"Yibambe!" everyone answered.

As the tribes of Wakanda, united under their king's Black Panther banner, stood alongside the Avengers, they watched in horror as thousands of Outriders—a race of four-armed, eyeless, and fanged humanoid creatures—began to emerge from the enemy vessels and rage forward, coming to an infuriated stop only when they reached the outskirts of the domed barrier. They clawed savagely at the barrier, cries echoing from their gaping maws.

"What the hell?" Bucky asked, horrified.

"Looks like we pissed her off," Natasha growled, taking in the brutal scene.

The Outriders continued to pour from the ships and threw themselves against the shield. They climbed on top of the bodies of their fallen and tried to force their way through the energy barrier, despite losing limbs and dying in the process.

Okoye stared in horror, standing by the Black Panther's side. "They're killing themselves." What she couldn't bring herself to say was that one by one, however slowly, they were breaking through Wakanda's defenses.

"Vala!" T'Challa commanded, telling his troops to *Lock!*

"Vala!" the troops answered. Following his command, they swept their protective capes in front of them as the Outrider onslaught advanced.

"*Kubo!*" T'Challa yelled, telling his troops to *Fire!*

"*Kubo!*" his troops rang back. They shot as one at the ravaging horde that threatened everything. As the Wakandan tribes' blue lasers shot across the field of battle, Bucky's weapon's bullets hit targets with brutal accuracy. Falcon soared overhead, taking in the horrific scene. An Outrider leaped up at him and Sam loosed three missiles in retaliation. Hitting all of his targets, he sailed past and called out to Rhodey. "You see the teeth on those things?" Sam asked, now having come way too close for comfort to one of the beasts.

"All right, back up, Sam. You're gonna get your wings singed," Rhodey warned, activating War Machine's grenades all along the barrier's perimeter.

"Cap, if these things circle the perimeter and get in behind us, there's nothing between them and Vision," Banner said.

"Then we better keep 'em in front of us." Cap eyed the barrier.

"How do we do that?" Okoye asked, definitely not wanting to hear the answer.

"We open the barrier," T'Challa said somberly. Putting his finger to his ear, he radioed back to headquarters. "On my signal, open Northwest Section Seventeen."

"Requesting confirmation, My King. You said, open the barrier?" his contact responded.

19

"On my signal." T'Challa's voice was calm.

"This will be the end of Wakanda," M'Baku said, scanning the battlefield.

"Then it will be the noblest ending in history," Okoye growled, steeling herself.

"Vula!" T'Challa commanded, the word simply meaning, *open.* His troops stood tall, deactivating their capes. T'Challa stepped forward.

"Wakanda Forever!" he yelled, crossing his arms across his chest as his face mask closed around his determined visage.

"Wakanda Forever!" the armies yelled as they ran toward the barrier as one unit, Captain America and the Black Panther the fastest among them.

"Now!" T'Challa yelled into the radio. And the barrier opened just as he commanded.

The two forces met with a wrenching crack. Chaos and blood rained down. Amid the snarling savagery that surrounded him, the Black Panther activated his comm, hailing his sister in the Wakandan Design Group lab. "How much longer, Shuri?"

Shuri looked to Vision on the lab table and the holographic image of the millions of neural pathways she would have to go through with surgical precision to succeed in extracting the Mind Stone.

"I've barely begun, brother," she replied earnestly, knowing how many lives hung in the balance.

Surveying the carnage already building up, T'Challa encouraged his sister. "You might want to pick up the pace."

On Nidavellir, Thor stepped inside the broken iris.

"All-Fathers, give me strength," Thor said. His voice was reverent and uncompromising. The sadness he'd felt for all he'd lost was momentarily transformed into a single-minded fixation. He needed that ax if he was going to kill Thanos. There was no other way.

"You understand, boy? You're about to take the full force of a star. It'll kill you," Eitri warned.

"Only if I die," Thor said, trying to buoy himself up in these last moments.

"Yes. That's what k-killing you means," Eitri answered, wondering if Thor understood the magnitude of what he was about to attempt.

Thor curled his fingers around one side of the iris and then the other. Without hesitation, he pulled both parts together as the beam of light shone bright behind him and then burst and raged through him, straight on through to the forge.

The forge erupted to life. Brilliant and powerful.

"Hold it! Hold it, Thor!" Eitri yelled as he checked the molten liquid now bubbling in the forge's once cold cauldrons. Eitri hurried over and shouldered the cauldron over, spilling the hot golden liquid into the molds just beneath. Just as the molten liquid spread across the Stormbreaker mold, Thor lost consciousness. Burned and near death, Thor's arms still hung on either side of the iris. When he finally collapsed, the power of the beam of light surged his slack and lifeless body toward the forge. Rocket took off in the pod, desperate to catch him.

"Oh!" Thor hit the side of the forge and rolled inside the docking bay, with Rocket close behind. Groot watched as Thor lay on the floor, motionless. Rocket leaped out of the pod and ran over to Thor. He knelt beside him and tried to shake him awake.

"Thor! Say somethin'. Come on. Thor, you okay?"

Eitri pulled the Stormbreaker off its platform and it broke apart. He pounded at the mold with his useless metal hands, trying to free the ax from its restraints. Rocket called out to Eitri in a desperate panic. "I think he's dyin'."

"He needs the ax. Where's the handle? Tree, help me find the handle!" Eitri ran through the forge in search of Stormbreaker's handle.

Groot looked over at Thor. At Rocket desperately trying to resuscitate the Thunder God. He thought about everything Thor had been willing to sacrifice just for the slightest chance of victory.

He set down his video game and steeled himself. It was time to be a part of this team.

Groot got up and walked over to Stormbreaker. The weapon was still glowing red from the heat and was split into two halves. He let his branches move and thread around the hammer and the ax. With a painful grunt, Groot finally pulled them both together. Groot dragged Stormbreaker to him, then lifted the legendary weapon high into the air, his arm now part of the weapon. With his other arm, he split his own arm apart from the ax, grimacing in pain.

Stormbreaker had found its handle.

Thor's fingers twitched as the weapon hit the floor of the forge. Blue sparks arched and sparked around Stormbreaker as it lifted off the floor, on its way to its new master.

The Outriders proved to be a single-minded foe: death to their enemies at any cost. Bucky, Steve, and the Black Panther fought in a rotating trio, but found themselves being pushed back farther from the domed shield.

The Outriders were undeterred by War Machine's bombs dropped from above.

Black Widow and Okoye slew as many as possible, covering each other's backs.

A half-dozen Outriders overcame the Hulkbuster armor, blinding Banner inside.

17

"There's too many of them!" Banner's voice broadcast to his fellow teammates, all of whom were experiencing the same situation since opening the gate.

For every hero, there were easily a thousand Outriders. They were losing badly.

Suddenly, the sky flashed a bright white and crackled with electricity just as a dozen bolts of lightning hit the ground. The energy from the bolts tore through a horde of Outriders, killing them instantly.

From inside the flash of light, Stormbreaker burst out across the Wakandan battlefield, killing hundreds more Outriders before curling back to its master.

Stepping out of the smoke, with Rocket on his shoulder and flanked by Groot, was the God of Thunder himself: Thor. Blue electricity sparked and laced around Thor as his red cape unfurled behind him.

Natasha and Cap looked at their old friend with relief and warmth. Thor was alive and here to help. Maybe all was not lost, after all.

"You guys are so screwed now!" Banner whooped from inside the Hulkbuster.

"Bring me Thanos!" Thor bellowed as he ran to the front line. Raising Stormbreaker, he launched himself high into the air in an explosive lightning storm. Soaring overhead, Thor's eyes glowing white, he descended onto the Outriders and began picking them off with speed and precision.

The tide had officially turned.

As he stepped through the teleportation portal, Thanos instantly felt there was something . . . off. He had been raised on Titan, and though it had been many years since he'd been cast out, it would always be his home. Right now, his home was telling him something was awry. Looking to his left, he saw the remains of Ebony Maw's ship, and his suspicions were confirmed. He spun at the sound of a sigh behind him.

"Oh, yeah." Doctor Stephen Strange was seated on a set of broken stairs leading nowhere, casually taking in the sight of the foe that had hunted him across the galaxy. "You're much more of a Thanos."

Thanos gave a heavy look to the keeper of the Time Stone. "I take it that Maw is dead?" Strange nodded yes. "This day extracts a heavy toll," Thanos sighed deeply. "Still, he accomplished his mission."

"You may regret that," Strange countered, the Eye of Agamotto glowing green in the presence of its fellow Stones. "He brought you face-to-face with the Master of the Mystic Arts."

"And where do you think he brought you?" Thanos asked.

16

Doctor Strange decided to play along. "Let me guess . . . your home?"

Thanos looked around, a strange sadness crossing his face. "It was," he said. He clenched the Gauntlet and the red of the Reality Stone shone bright. Suddenly Strange and Thanos were seated in the heart of the city when it was thriving. Bright skies, ships floating, a busy metropolitan mecca.

"And it was beautiful."

Strange tried to cover the awe that he felt in seeing the Reality Stone in use. Instead, he focused on Thanos, who was lost in the past that once more walked about him like a ghost.

"Titan was like most planets. Too many mouths, not enough to go around." He sounded frustrated. "And when we faced extinction, I offered a solution."

"Genocide." Strange did not mince words.

"But random," Thanos agreed, to Strange's shock. "Dispassionate. Fair to rich and poor alike. They called me a madman. And what I predicted came to pass." Thanos unflexed the Gauntlet and reality returned to Titan.

"Congratulations, you're a prophet," Strange said sarcastically.

"I'm a survivor."

"Who wants to murder trillions," Strange said, going toe-to-toe with Thanos.

"With all six Stones, I could simply snap my fingers. They would all cease to exist." He looked at Strange as if the mystic would understand his point of view as well. "I call that mercy."

Strange stood up and walked toward Thanos, interested in getting as much information from him as possible. "And then what?"

"I'd finally rest and watch the sun rise on a grateful universe. The hardest choices require the strongest wills," he explained.

"I think you'll find our will equal to yours." Strange conjured up two golden protective mandalas.

A fleeting look of surprise crossed Thanos's face. "'Our'?"

On cue, Iron Man pushed a massive broken column down onto Thanos.

"Piece of cake, Quill," Tony called out, soaring around the wreckage.

"Yeah, if your goal was to piss him off." Quill activated his face mask and took off after Stark.

A burst of purple energy exploded from beneath the massive broken column. Thanos howled as the Power Stone shone bright. Then with another twist of the Gauntlet, the red Reality Stone turned the broken column's rubble into a flock of bats, which he immediately commanded to attack the completely caught off-guard Iron Man.

As Thanos watched Iron Man carried off, both of his

15

eyes were blinded by some kind of webbing. This offered just enough time for Drax to drop in, both knives drawn, and slash Thanos at the knees.

The combined Guardians and Avengers attacked a shocked Thanos. Repulsor blasts, webs, magical swords and ropes, blasters, daggers, blow after blow to keep the Mad Titan off balance.

"Boom," said Star-Lord flying overhead. Thanos looked up in time to see Quill wave goodbye, and then an explosion rocked the ground beneath the Titan.

Strange, wielding a magical rope that was pulling Thanos's wrist back, ordered the Cloak of Levitation to attack as well. "Don't let him close his fist!" he ordered, and the Cloak surrounded the Infinity Gauntlet.

As the heroes ganged up, they managed to bring Thanos down to one knee. A portal opened by his head and Spider-Man came flying out, fist first.

"Magic!" he exclaimed as he hit Thanos, then vanished through another portal. A second pair of portals opened and Spidey flipped through, webbing Thanos's face and pulling as he disappeared, yelling, "More magic!"

A third pair opened and Spider-Man kicked Thanos, driving him farther down. "Magic with a kick!"

A fourth pair opened. "Magic with a—" This time Thanos was waiting for Spider-Man. He grabbed him around his neck and blasted the boy into the ground with such force that it left a crater where his body met the unyielding earth.

"Insect," Thanos growled as Peter squirmed beneath his iron grip. Thanos picked up the boy and hurled him directly into Strange. Thanos ripped the Cloak off his Gauntlet-covered hand just as Tony flew in with explosive force. A force Thanos's Gauntlet sucked up and then aimed right back at Iron Man. Spider-Man used his web-shooters to try to once again disable the Gauntlet, but Thanos ripped the webbing from the golden glove and sent Peter hurtling through the air in reply. As Thanos watched Peter soar, an unknown ship whizzed past Thanos, hitting him as it crash-landed.

As Thanos rose to one knee, Nebula sailed over him and threw a single punch at her father's face before coming to land in front of him, her sword already drawn.

"Well, well," he muttered, visibly impressed.

"You should've killed me," Nebula sneered.

Thanos barked back, "It would have been a waste of parts." Nebula struck him across the face again without hesitation.

"Where's Gamora?" she demanded.

Thanos hit Nebula with the back of his hand, sending her flying.

It was time for the team to take the best shot they would get.

14

In the moments that followed, Strange wrapped Thanos's Gauntleted hand in red energy ropes, pulling the fingers straight. Drax slid in and kicked Thanos, so the Titan fell to his knees. Quill electrified Thanos's other hand, so that it stretched out toward the ground. Spider-Man swung around the Titan, using his webs to lasso him in place. Tony dropped down and wrapped his hands around the Gauntlet.

They had him, which meant it was time for the most critical part of the attack. A portal opened above Thanos's head and Mantis dropped onto his shoulders and placed her hands on his temples. He fought, but Mantis was able to establish an empathetic connection with Thanos.

His shoulders slumped as his eyes closed.

"Is he under? Don't let up," Iron Man ordered.

"Be quick. He is very strong," Mantis said, straining to maintain her hold on him.

"Parker, help. Get over here. She can't hold him much longer. Let's go." Peter fell in next to Tony and together they struggled to pull the Gauntlet off Thanos's hand.

"Again, again, again. I'll push on three. Go." The two pulled and tugged as they worked together.

"Cool! Let's move," Tony said to Peter as they felt the slightest give.

"We gotta open his fingers to get it off," Peter said, his voice a strained grunt.

Quill landed in front of Thanos, gloating. "I thought you'd be harder to catch. For the record, this was my plan," he boasted, walking toward him. "Not so strong now, huh?"

Thanos groaned, mentally trying to break free.

"Where is Gamora?" Quill demanded.

"Mu-mu-my Ga-Gamora . . ." Thanos croaked out. This only angered Peter Quill more.

"No lies! Where is she?"

Mantis began to sway on Thanos's shoulders, her face contorting in pain. "He is in anguish," she said.

"Good," Quill shot back.

Mantis shook her head as Thanos's pain filled her. "He . . . he mourns."

"What does this monster have to mourn?" Drax grunted, still struggling to hold Thanos down.

"Gamora," spoke a sorrowful voice from behind them.

Quill turned to face Nebula, the speaker, confusion on his face. "What?"

Nebula's gaze was trained on Thanos as she spoke, examining his expressions, praying she was wrong even while knowing she wasn't. "He took her to Vormir. He came back with the Soul Stone . . ." Her voice dropped to a whisper. "But she didn't."

Sensing where this was going, Tony receded his face mask and started talking as fast as he could.

13

"Okay, Quill, you gotta cool it right now. You understand? Don't, don't, don't engage." Quill turned to face Thanos and, desperate, Tony barked, "We almost got this off!"

"Tell me she's lying. Tell me you didn't do it!" Quill's face flushed in anger, his eyes were rimmed in red, the tears already welling in their depths.

Thanos forced out the words, "I had to."

Quill shook his head in disbelief. "No, you didn't. No, you didn't." Star-Lord whipped out his blaster and slammed it across Thanos's face. "NO. NO, YOU DIDN'T!"

"Quill!" Tony lunged into Quill, making him stop hitting Thanos. "Hey, stop!"

"It's comin', it's comin'—" Spider-Man said, the Gauntlet pulling away from Thanos's hand more and more.

"Hey! Stop, stop!" Tony fought with Quill, desperate to keep their plan on track.

"It's comin'—" Peter said through gritted teeth.

"Hey! Stop, stop!" Tony repeated with desperation. He wrapped himself around Quill's arm as he heard Peter getting closer and closer. Just a little bit longer. Just a little bit longer.

And then it worked.

Peter pulled the Gauntlet about an inch off Thanos's hand. "I got it! I got it!"

Thanos's eyes snapped open and his fingers curled

around the Gauntlet, pulling it back from Peter's grip. Thanos reached up to Mantis and hurled her as far away from his shoulders as possible.

"Oh, God . . ." Spider-Man took off after Mantis, catching her before she hit the ground.

One by one, Thanos made quick work of the remaining Avengers and Guardians. A purple energy rippled out from his Gauntlet, knocking out Quill, Drax, and Nebula all at once.

As Tony blasted Thanos, the Titan decided to handle this gnat once and for all. Thanos looked to the sky, made a fist with the Gauntlet, and sent an energy blast high into the air. Looking up, Iron Man paled.

The moon Thanos had summoned with the Infinity Stones was crashing down around them.

12

CHAPTER 12

11

The battle of Wakanda raged on and, while Thor's arrival had bought the Avengers and the Wakandans some time, there was still no end in sight. Cull Obsidian slashed through the Wakandan ranks with his hammer, and it took the Black Panther himself to stall the Child of Thanos for even just a moment.

"Come and get some, space dogs!" Rocket taunted as he spun around and shot at any Outrider that came near. Next to him, Bucky saw an opportunity. Picking Rocket up, he spun the shooting raccoon around in a rapid circle as he took care of whoever charged them on his side. "Come on! Get some! Get some! Get some! Come on, get some!" Rocket yelled as they wiped out an entire mile-wide circumference. Bucky set down the raccoon with a nod of thanks.

"How much for the gun?" Rocket asked.

"Not for sale," Bucky answered.

"Okay. How much for the arm?" Bucky gave Rocket a bemused look before walking off in search of his next victim. "Oh, I'll get that arm," Rocket muttered after him with a grin.

Thor swung Stormbreaker, taking out countless Outriders. In a brief lull, he looked across the battlefield to see Cap.

"New haircut?" Steve asked, breathless.

"Noticed you've copied my beard?"

Cap nodded, still trying to catch his breath.

Behind them, Groot impaled three Outriders. Thor said, "By the way, this is a friend of mine, Tree."

"I am Groot!" Groot said, holding up the three impaled Outriders.

"I am Steve Rogers," Cap said, putting his hand on his chest as introduction.

Just when the Avengers and Wakandans felt they'd started to get a handle on the battle, Thanos's army unleashed another nasty surprise: great war machines taller than the highest trees in the forest rolled out, spiked gears mauling everything in their way.

"Fall back!" T'Challa commanded. "Fall back now!" He needed to get his troops to safety.

From the tower above, Wanda had watched the battle unfold. She knew Shuri needed more time to remove the Mind Stone, and over the comms she heard the Black Panther give the orders to fall back.

"Focus that fire on the left flank, Sam," War Machine commanded.

"I'm doin' it," Sam answered as the two men focused on taking out as many of these great rolling spikes as they could.

10

As Okoye and Black Widow fought, they didn't notice a rolling spike coming right their way. Just as they both braced for impact, Wanda landed in front of them and used her red energy bolts to lift the giant machine over the allies and right on top of the Outrider army behind them.

Okoye turned to Black Widow, flipping her staff around in her hand. "Why was she up there all this time?"

Across the stream, well hidden, Proxima Midnight spoke into her comm. "She's on the field. Take it."

In the lab, Shuri and her Dora Milaje guard, Ayo, were shocked at the sudden entrance of Corvus Glaive, who was apparently not dead after all. Ayo and Glaive's battle rang throughout the lab as Shuri worked twice as fast to try to sever the connections between the Mind Stone and Vision.

Deep down, Vision knew this was not their battle. This was his own unfinished business. So, when Corvus Glaive made his way to Shuri after overpowering Ayo, Vision stood suddenly and tackled the lean alien. He propelled himself and Corvus Glaive to a window and the pair crashed through, falling to the ground below.

Using his long-range vision goggles, Falcon saw the duo's fall from across the battlefield. His palms instantly began to sweat.

"Guys," Falcon radioed, "we got a Vision situation here."

Steve was surrounded by Outriders, kicking and shield-bashing them at every turn. He yelled into his comm, "Somebody get to Vision!"

"I got him!" Banner answered, speeding toward Vision.

"On my way," Wanda said, just before she was smacked across the face with Proxima's staff, sending her rolling into a nearby ditch. Proxima turned Wanda over and loomed above her.

"He'll die alone. As will you," Proxima tormented.

"She's not alone," said a raspy, calm voice from behind Proxima. Proxima turned to see Black Widow. She turned back around to see Okoye spinning her staff around. Both were ready for a fight. Okoye gave Natasha a nod, but it was Proxima who lunged first. Black Widow and Okoye threaded and moved around Proxima, their movements so precise and lethal it was as if they had been choreographed.

Banner finally caught up to Vision, just in time to see Cull Obsidian deliver a massive blow to the superbot, sending him reeling. Bruce settled in across from Corvus and Cull.

"This isn't gonna be like New York, pal," Banner

9

warned. "This suit's already kicked the crap outta the Hulk." Cull latched onto Banner and launched himself and Banner through the woods and far away from Vision and Corvus Glaive.

"Guys, Vision needs backup now!" Banner radioed as he and Cull smashed against the side of a waterfall. "Hulk? Hulk? I know you like making your entrance at the last second. Well, this is it, man. This, this, is the last, last second."

Cull responded by using his mechanical hammer to smash one of the arms on the Hulkbuster armor, wrapping the chain around it. Cull pulled the armor off.

"Oh, no. Ah! Hulk! Hulk! Hulk!" Banner called.

"Noooooo!" Hulk responded.

"Oh, screw you, you big green jerk. I'll do it myself." Banner lunged at Cull Obsidian and after a brutal back-and-forth, slid his own detached Hulkbuster arm onto Cull Obsidian. Banner pressed a button and Cull's eyes widened in alarm as the repulsor ignited.

"See ya!" Bruce waved. The Hulkbuster's repulsor carried Cull Obsidian high into the air until he collided with the domed shield. The alien exploded on impact.

"Hulk, we got a lot to figure out, pal," Banner said, finally able to catch his breath.

But things were only getting worse. Just as it looked

like Proxima had bested both Natasha and Okoye, Corvus Glaive ran his spear through Vision.

"I thought you were formidable, machine. But you're dying, like any man." Corvus pulled his blade from Vision with one cruel tug. Vision collapsed at Corvus's feet. As Corvus bent over Vision to begin the process of extracting the Mind Stone, Captain America managed to reach the pair and tackle Corvus Glaive to the ground.

"Get out of here!" Cap yelled to Vision as he parried against Corvus Glaive, spear against shield, hand to hand, outright brawling. "Go!"

Vision struggled to get to his feet.

Wanda needed to finish this fight and get to Vision. This was precious time, and she'd wasted enough of it on Proxima to last a lifetime. The Scarlet Witch heard a by-now-familiar sound approaching. Red energy began to rise from her hands, and one of the war machines rose from the ground behind her, soared over her head, and rolled right over Proxima Midnight.

All three women looked away as blue liquid from their enemy splattered them.

"That was really gross," Black Widow sighed, wiping the alien blood from her arm.

Steve managed to disarm Glaive, but in the process had given higher ground to his foe, who sprung upon

8

the soldier. His long fingers wrapped themselves around Steve's neck and began to squeeze. Gasping for air, Steve reached for anything to beat the villain back, but he was beginning to lose consciousness.

Suddenly, he saw the last thing he expected: the curved end of Corvus Glaive's own spear emerging from his chest. The foe gasped, lost his grasp on Steve, and was lifted into the air by his own blade.

Steve saw it was Vision wielding the spear, in a reversal of the fight that had torn Vision's own side in Scotland. With a final gasp, Corvus Glaive went limp. Vision tossed the final member of the Children of Thanos to the side and struggled to stay standing after his own fall and fight with Glaive moments earlier.

"I thought I told you to go," Steve gasped.

Bracing himself against a nearby tree stump, Vision gave a weak smile and repeated Steve's earlier words back to him.

"We don't trade lives, Captain."

The moon had broken into meteors when Thanos pulled it from its orbit and brought it crashing onto the surface of Titan. The destruction had ravaged the remaining gravitational balance, not to mention the toll it took on the heroes that had faced Thanos.

Of everyone that had fought him, only Doctor Strange still stood conscious. With a circular motion, Strange cast a spell that encased Thanos in a crystal prison. Thanos smirked as he used the Reality and Power Stones to break the prison into a thousand shards and send them flying back at the Master of the Mystic Arts. Strange countered by creating a shield that turned the shards into a multitude of blue butterflies upon impact.

Quickly recovering, he cast a spell that split his image into dozens of identical copies, each wielding eldritch whips. They struck as one, hundreds of whips entwining Thanos from every angle.

Thanos, not fooled, gripped a single cord and yanked hard. All of the images collapsed back into one: Doctor Strange's true form. The mystic kneeled, stunned.

"You're full of tricks, wizard," Thanos said, grabbing the dazed mystic by the neck. "Yet you never once used your greatest weapon."

His gaze turned to the Eye of Agamotto hanging around Strange's neck. Thanos grabbed it and crushed the mystical artifact in his bare hand. The amulet shattered easily.

"A fake." Thanos smiled at Strange's cleverness . . . for a moment. His eyes hardened and he flung Doctor Strange into a pile of rubble. Walking to him, Thanos

7

raised the Gauntlet and aimed it at Strange's head, only to find something blaze past and stick to his palm, making it impossible to close.

"You throw another moon at me and I'm gonna lose it," Iron Man said, squaring off one more time against the Titan.

"Stark," Thanos growled.

Iron Man was taken aback for a moment. "You know me?"

"I do. You're not the only one cursed with knowledge."

Apparently, Tony thought, he had been haunting the Titan's thoughts for the past six years as well. That gave him a slight bit of joy. "My only curse is you."

With that, Iron Man's shoulder missile launchers rose, clicked into place, and fired. Thanos blocked them all with the Gauntlet's power.

"Come on!" Thanos challenged, crushing the device that briefly inhibited the Gauntlet.

But for every missile landed, every beam fired and blocked, every punch countered, Thanos outmatched Iron Man. With the power of the Stones he was too much for one person. Slowly, painfully, Tony's nanite suit was stripped away or torn apart by the power of the Infinity Stones. In the process, Tony landed one good kick to Thanos's face.

"All that for a drop of blood," Thanos mused, wiping at the scratch with his finger. The payback for this blood-letting, albeit minimal, was fierce and immediate. Thanos wrenched his arm up and punched Tony hard, flipping him through the air. Another punch. And another. Tony was being ground down, one body blow at a time.

In a last-ditch effort, Tony formed a makeshift sword from a piece of debris and swung it at Thanos. The villain grabbed the sword and jabbed it into Tony's side, twisting it for added pain.

Thanos walked Tony back, until he finally stumbled into a seated position on a loose piece of rubble. Thanos placed his Gauntleted hand on top of Stark's head. "You have my respect, Stark. When I'm done, half of humanity will still be alive." Tony stifled a moan of pain. "I hope they remember you," Thanos said as a stream of blood dripped down from Tony's mouth. He raised the Gauntlet and pointed it at the unarmored and defenseless Tony Stark.

"Stop."

Pulling himself from the rubble, Stephen Strange struggled to sit up. "Spare his life and I will give you the Stone."

This came as a shock to both Tony and Thanos.

"No tricks," demanded Thanos.

6

Strange shook his head. No tricks.

"Don't," Tony gasped at Strange, mustering everything he had to protest. He and Strange had a deal. Strange had the moral compass. He'd promised.

Strange gave his ally a knowing look before gazing to the heavens. He reached up and appeared to pinch a star in the distance. Instantly, it grew and began to glow emerald. The Time Stone, hidden the whole time in plain sight. Tony winced in pain at the sight of the Time Stone.

The Stone flew from Strange's hand into Thanos's. He gently held it above the knuckle piece in the Gauntlet and dropped it in. With a rush of energy, the power of the five Stones washed over Thanos. He breathed it in and then looked down at the sole empty spot on the glove.

"One to go," Thanos said and vanished. Just then Peter Quill rounded the corner, firing his blaster into the space Thanos had just occupied.

"Where is he?" Quill panted. Looking around, he saw that Thanos was nowhere to be seen. "Did we just lose?"

Stark pulled the blade from his side, muffling his cry of pain. Nanites quickly began to stitch the wound, but he was still in critical condition. Nonetheless, he stared at Strange in disbelief. The Keeper of the Stone had traded it . . . for Stark's life?!

"Why? Why would you do that?" Tony was baffled, but Strange's look in return was one of resolve as he answered.

"We're in the endgame now."

5

CHAPTER 13

4

With their leaders defeated, the Outriders were quickly rounded up and destroyed by the Wakandans and the Avengers. Thor flew across the fields of battle wielding Stormbreaker, cleansing the land with lightning.

In the forest clearing, Vision was struggling to stand. Wanda helped him to his feet.

"Are you okay?" she asked.

Vision winced, touching the Mind Stone. "He's here," was the only answer Vision could give.

Steve Rogers, alerted by Vision's words, spoke into his comm. "Everyone on my position. We have incoming."

The air was eerily still. After the largest-scale battle Earth had seen in a single day in decades, the silence was deafening. Black Widow, Falcon, T'Challa, Okoye, and Banner all made their way to Steve's position.

An unearthly movement in the air caught Natasha's gaze. "What the hell?" Black smoke appeared from what looked like a tear in the middle of the air. Through it stepped the massive Titan, Thanos. Banner's breath caught in his throat.

"Cap. That's him."

That was all the confirmation Steve needed. "Eyes up. Stay sharp."

Banner leaped to attack, but Thanos used the power of

the Stones to cause Bruce to pass through him, then phase into the rock wall behind Thanos.

After that, one at a time the heroes rushed to Thanos only to be tossed aside or blown back by an energy wave. Vision saw all of this and knew what must be done. He only hoped Wanda could trust him.

"Wanda, it's time," Vision said, his voice pained and constricted.

"No," Wanda said, still standing, ready to fight. Her voice was defiant. She was not having this conversation. There was another way. There had to be another way.

"They can't stop him, Wanda, but we can." Vision reached up and pulled Wanda to him. "Look at me. You have the power to destroy the Stone."

"Don't." Wanda remained standing, at the ready to fight. Still convinced there was some other way than the plan Vision was proposing.

"You must do it. Wanda, please." Vision curled his fingers around her hand and placed it on his face. Making her stop. See him. This was the only way. "We are out of time."

Wanda shook her head, her eyes filling with tears. "I can't."

"Yes, you can. You can." Vision lifted her hand and placed it in front of his forehead. "If he gets the Stone, half the universe dies." He looked deep in her eyes. "It's not fair. It shouldn't be you, but it is. It's all right."

3

Wanda backed away from him, her hand still raised. Vision's voice grew calmer as he sensed his end drawing near. "You could never hurt me."

A wave of acceptance washed over Wanda as she finally recognized what she must do.

Vision locked eyes with her. His voice was soft and loving as he spoke. "I just feel you."

With a swirl of energy, Wanda took a deep breath and began to use her powers to destroy the Stone and, with it, the love of her life.

She forced herself to keep eye contact with Vis, wanting her face to be the final thing he saw as he lived his last few moments on Earth. But as time wore on she found it unbearable to watch as the life slowly drained from Vision. For a brief moment, she looked away. Her heart breaking, tears streaming down her face, Wanda grew more and more hysterical.

Looking back over at Vis, she needed to make his pain come to an end. She needed to give him one last act of true love. Wanda brought up her other hand and doubled up the energy now aimed at the Stone. Vis would feel no pain soon. He would be free from all of this. At least she could give him that. Vis closed his eyes and let Wanda's energy move through him.

Close by, each hero took his or her turn against Thanos, and each was met with swift defeat. Bucky, Okoye, Widow, all rushed toward him or fired upon him only to have their weapons halted or turned back on them. Steve Rogers ran at Thanos from behind and slid on his knees, hitting the Titan in the leg. Thanos was surprised someone actually landed a blow. He lifted his Gauntleted hand, made a fist, and swung down to crush the nuisance before him. To his shock, Steve Rogers caught the fist in both hands, stopping it. Teeth gritting, he pushed back at Thanos. Even the villain was impressed . . . before landing a blow with his other fist that sent Steve flying.

The Scarlet Witch's powers were causing the Mind Stone to finally crack slightly. She heard Thanos approaching from behind her and split her focus, blasting Thanos with one hand while intent on destroying the Stone with energy from the other.

Wanda threw up an energy barrier that bought them enough time for her to focus on Vision. The final moments were at hand and they both knew it.

"It's all right," Vision whispered, his eyes locked on hers. Wanda poured all of her energy into destroying the Mind Stone. "It's all right," Vision repeated.

Outside the barrier, Thanos bashed the energy field with the Gauntlet, but it barely dented. He had come so far, and the final piece was slipping through his fingers before him.

The Mind Stone began to crackle suddenly, finally

2

reaching critical damage. As Wanda sobbed, Vision spoke, his voice intimate and tender. "I love you." Her cries burst from her as Vis's eyes closed. His face was calm and serene as the Mind Stone shattered. Yellow energy shot out and washed over everyone. Vision collapsed, his entire body ashen gray.

"I understand, my child," came Thanos's voice as he approached Wanda. "Better than anyone."

Wanda's eyes flared. "You could never!"

To her surprise, Thanos looked softly at her. "Today I lost more than you can know." He walked to stand beside the lifeless body of Vision. "But now is no time to mourn. Now is no time at all."

Forming a fist with the Gauntlet, a magical green ring appeared around Thanos's wrist. He had activated the Time Stone, reversing time. Wanda weeping, the destruction of the Stone, Vision's declaration of love, all played back in reverse until Vision stood before him, Mind Stone intact and on his forehead.

"No!" Wanda screamed, but was blasted across the clearing by Thanos.

The Titan faced Vision and gripped him by the throat. He lifted him and pried out the Mind Stone from his forehead. Vision's forehead crumbled and his body went limp. Thanos threw him aside.

Holding the Mind Stone above the final bezel over the

vacant knuckle of the Infinity Gauntlet, Thanos dropped it into place. Instantly, cosmic energy that had not been collected in a single place since before the Big Bang washed over him and coursed through him.

Thanos arched his back and bellowed. He raised his fist and the energy began to dissipate.

All six Stones were pulsating in unison now. He stared at them, so transfixed he never saw the lightning bolt aimed for his chest hit him square in the center, sending him tumbling and crashing through a copse of trees.

Thor appeared and raised Stormbreaker. Before Thanos could react, Thor hurled Stormbreaker end over end until it found its mark in Thanos's chest, embedding there with a dull thud.

Thor walked to the Titan, who was struggling to find breath.

"I told you you'd die for that." Thor pushed Stormbreaker deeper into Thanos's chest, causing him to stifle a cry of pain.

Panting for air, Thanos met Thor's gaze and smiled, privy to a joke only he knew the punchline to.

"You . . . should have . . . gone . . . for the head." Thanos gasped as he raised his hand. Thor saw the Infinity Gauntlet on it, all six Stones glowing. Thanos gave a bigger grin as Thor's eyes widened in horror.

"NO!"

THANOS SNAPPED HIS FINGERS.

CHAPTER 14

Thanos, the Gauntlet no longer on his hand and dressed in a tunic, stepped out of a simple structure, shallow water surrounding him. He was no longer on Earth. In fact, he wasn't sure where he was.

A noise made him turn. He saw a young, green-skinned child approach him.

"Daughter?"

"Did you do it?" she asked.

"Yes."

"What did it cost?"

With a heavy sigh, he answered. "Everything."

As quickly as his mind had drifted, it snapped back to focus and he was on Earth again, in Wakanda, Thor above him.

Thanos looked at the Infinity Gauntlet, which was burnt and cracked now, but the Stones still glowed. A teleportation portal opened behind him and Thanos vanished from Earth, leaving the inhabitants to discover the consequences of his actions. Stormbreaker dropped to the ground as the portal closed.

"What did you do?" yelled Thor, but Thanos was gone.

Steve came running in. "Where did he go?" he asked Thor, but the Asgardian had no response. "Thor. Where did he go?"

Bucky's voice interrupted as he entered the clearing,

walking strangely. "Steve?" Before he could say more, he dropped his gun and turned to dust, blipped out of existence. Steve ran to where his friend had been, but there was no sign Bucky Barnes had been in that spot except the ashes left.

M'Baku watched helplessly as his fellow Wakandan warriors and citizens turned to dust around him.

"Up, General, up! This is no place to die." T'Challa was helping Okoye to her feet as he started to turn to dust. When he was gone, Okoye fell to the ground, searching frantically for her king.

In the clearing near Okoye, Rocket sat by Groot, who was painlessly and ever so quietly turning to dust in front of him. "I am Groot," he said weakly.

"Oh. No . . . n-no, no, no! Groot!" Just as Rocket reached out to embrace his closest friend, Groot turned to ash in his hands. "No!" Rocket cried out as his heart broke, the ashes of Groot settling all around him.

Wanda held Vision's lifeless body in her arms, and as she turned to dust, she smiled. Relieved that she didn't have to endure one more second on this planet without her love.

All by himself, Falcon struggled to stand, turning to dust before anyone knew where he'd landed. Alone and afraid, his ashes drifted along on the Wakandan winds.

"Sam?" Rhodey called out, running to him but not

making it in time. "Sam? Where you at?" Rhodey called out again.

No one answered.

Across the galaxy on Titan, Mantis looked up.

"Something's happening," she warned just before turning into dust. Tony watched in horror as Drax looked up.

"Quill?" Drax said, just before turning to dust, his ashes now part of the dusty ruins of Titan. Quill looked to Tony in horror.

"Steady, Quill," Tony eased, walking toward him. Quill looked at his arms, and must have felt something because he managed to utter "Oh, man," before turning to dust himself.

From the rubble of the stairs, Doctor Strange called to Iron Man. "Tony." He made sure Tony was paying attention. "There was no other way." With that, he turned to dust as well.

"Mr. Stark?" Peter Parker's voice was weak and scared. "I don't feel so good." *No,* Tony thought. *Please, no. Not him.* Peter stumbled toward Tony, his arms outstretched. Tony rushed to Peter. "You're all right," Tony assured him, just like he'd done before.

"I don't know what's happening. I don't know." Peter fell into Tony's arms and Tony wrapped his arms tightly around the boy. Peter held on to Tony and began to cry. He was just a kid. Tony held him as he sobbed. "I don't wanna go. I don't wanna go, sir. Please. Please. I don't want to go. I don't want to go." Peter fell to the ground and Tony with him. Peter's arm was still tight around Tony's neck.

Tony leaned in. *Look at me, kid. I'm calm. You're going to be okay,* he thought. *I'm right here. I'm right here. Just look at me.* Tony grasped Peter's shoulder, his eyes locked on his as, with a tiny whisper, Peter turned to dust.

"I'm sorry." Tony slammed his hand through where Peter once was. His hand now full of nothing but ashes. Tony willed it to be false. Willed the boy back. Willed another chance to save him. To be there for him. To protect him. To love him.

"He did it." Nebula's voice came from behind Tony. He had forgotten she was still there. At least in this decaying part of the universe he wasn't completely alone, Tony thought. Then it struck him—what Nebula said. Thanos had achieved what he'd set out to do—to balance the universe, at any cost.

Pepper. Had Pepper survived? How much had he truly lost?

Captain America rolled Vision over and assessed the damage to his friend just as Natasha ran up.

"What is this?" Rhodey asked, looking around at the remaining five Avengers: Thor, Banner, Natasha, Cap, and himself. "What the hell is happening?"

Sitting next to Vision's gray, discolored corpse, Cap began putting the pieces together. His face paled and his entire body deflated.

"Oh, God," Cap said as he realized what Thanos had done.

Somewhere on a planet far away, the sun was rising. Thanos sat on the front steps outside a simple hut as the rays of dawn hit his face. For the first time since he could remember, the Titan's face lit in a genuine smile.

Thanos had won.

EPILOGUE

"Still no word from Stark?" Nick Fury asked.

"No, not yet. We're watching every satellite on both hemispheres, but still nothing," Maria Hill said as she scanned her device for answers.

"What is it?" Fury asked.

"Multiple bogeys over Wakanda," Hill said urgently.

"Same energy signal as New York?"

"Ten times bigger." Maria's tone was serious.

"Tell Klein we'll meet him—"

Just then a black SUV screeched around, crashing just in front of them.

"Nick! Nick!" Maria yelled, pointing at the spinning vehicle.

Fury hopped out of the car with Hill. She walked up to the black SUV.

"They okay?" Fury asked after the driver.

"There's no one here," Hill said, meeting his eyes, her voice scared and spiraling.

Above, a helicopter crashed into a building. The city was in absolute chaos. It was worse than the Chitauri, worse than Ultron.

"Call control. Code red," Fury ordered.

But Hill didn't answer. "Nick," she said, her voice soft. Nick Fury turned in time to see his partner turn to dust.

"Oh, no." Nick took out an old-school 1990s-era pager

and punched in a sequence of digits just as he saw his own hand turn to dust.

"Mother—" Fury sighed just as he disappeared.

The device fell to the ground, flashing the word SENDING . . . SENDING . . . Finally, it connected. The device lit up.

On the display was a red, blue, and yellow insignia. If anyone saw it, they might not have recognized it. But to those who knew, it meant only one thing: someone had received the call for help.

THE END